FULL CIRCLE

SHERLOCK HOLMES'S GREATEST
CHALLENGE EVER

A novella by
Maurice Breslow

 FriesenPress

One Printers Way
Altona, MB R0G 0B0
Canada

www.friesenpress.com

Copyright © 2022 Maurice Breslow
First Edition — 2022

All rights reserved.

No part of this publication may be reproduced in any form, or by any means, electronic or mechanical, including photocopying, recording, or any information browsing, storage, or retrieval system, without permission in writing from FriesenPress.

ISBN
978-1-03-913708-0 (Hardcover)
978-1-03-913707-3 (Paperback)
978-1-03-913709-7 (eBook)

1. FICTION, MYSTERY & DETECTIVE

Distributed to the trade by The Ingram Book Company

TO

MEG, MIMI, MAX and ABBE

ACKNOWLEDGMENTS

My thanks and gratitude to my wife Margaret, my daughter Miriam, and to Joan Harcourt, who generously gave their time and talent to read *Full Circle* at various stages in its development, and offered many useful comments and suggestions. Their input and encouragement contributed greatly to whatever merits the finished story possesses.

I also wish to thank Janet Layberry, my editor at Friesen Press, for her painstaking and insightful reading of the completed manuscript of *Full Circle*. Her perceptive observations and suggestions were an invaluable help in bringing the novella to its final form.

The novella *Full Circle* is adapted from the author's stage play of the same name. Copies of the play, as well as its amateur production rights, may be obtained by contacting Playwrights Guild of Canada (playwrightsguild.ca; telephone 416-703-0201). Professional production rights are available through the author, who can be contacted through Playwrights Guild of Canada.

FULL CIRCLE

Sherlock Holmes's Greatest
Challenge Ever

I

could not for the life of me say how it was that shortly after five o'clock of a bright early-autumn day, Holmes and I found ourselves in a rural precinct of Surrey, proceeding as if propelled by an unseen hand down a byway called Tennison Road, and whisked into the large, gabled, red-brick house that stood at number 12. Drawn at once into a spacious room, the curtains of which had been tightly closed against the late-afternoon sun, we saw a gentleman and two ladies seated around a table with their hands joined. At the centre of the table burned a single candle. Lingering on the air, a woman's voice, barely discernible, intoned, "Charles Doyle, are you here? Charles Doyle … are you with us? Your son Arthur … your daughter-in-law Louise … 'Touie'… wish to…"

At this point we stepped forward, the better to make out what was taking place, when at once we found ourselves confronted by a shout of "There! There!" and the gentleman pointing straight at us. "Look! There!" We froze, then at once stepped back beyond the reach of the candlelight. From there I saw one of the women, who from her attitude and place at the table seemed to be in command of the occasion, make a sharp gesture as if to hold us in our place. Which it did.

"Where, Arthur?" asked the other woman, looking in our general direction. She took hold of his arm. "What do you see? Is it your father?"

"Father? No, Touie. Not Father. It's…" The man shook his head vigorously, as if to clear it. "Do you not see them?!"

"What is it, sir?" asked the first woman, who was strikingly—one might even say exotically—attired in a flowing garment of purple and turquoise, with a similarly coloured turban on her head, rings on her fingers and ears, and bracelets on her wrists. For all that, she seemed to me vaguely familiar. But any ruminations on that score were forestalled by my noticing that from her hand dangled a light chain necklace and oval-shaped pendant, catching the candle's glow so that it itself appeared to be radiating light. This curious object she now slipped into the pocket of her garment. "See whom?" she asked the gentleman.

"Them!" he exclaimed. "THEM!" He stared into the shadows that held Holmes and myself, then started in our direction. Again we tensed, but suddenly the man stopped, as if dumbfounded. "His stick!" he said. "Is that his…?" His attention turned now to a walking stick leaning against the wall not far from where we stood. He studied it a few seconds. "It *is,*" the gentleman continued, eyes still on the walking stick. "Of course it is. It was he … they … that I saw." He turned back towards us and peered. At once, the turbaned lady made the same sharp gesture as before. "Gone," he said. "They're gone."

We were there still.

He was looking straight at us, but saw us not. *How can this be? I wondered. Is it the shadows in the room? I shouldn't think so.* I even had the distinctly uncomfortable notion that we were in some elaborate dream, but at once dismissed that thought. In its place came the feeling of wonder I'd already experienced during our odd, unbidden journey to this place.

At that moment, however, my thoughts were interrupted by the woman called Touie. "Who, Arthur?" she asked. I heard deep concern in her voice. "*Who* is gone?"

"I…" The gentleman shook his head in consternation. "I don't know, my dear. I thought I…" Again he shook his head. "I don't know."

She hesitated, then turned to the turbaned lady. "Madame Eneri, perhaps for now"—she moved to usher her out of the room—"it's best we—"

"Are you sure?" the other woman asked. "I've had experience with occurrences of this sort."

"No, please, Madame. My husband's been under some strain lately." As she said this, she looked at the gentleman, who had not budged from his previous position. "No more, Arthur," his wife said. "We'll do no more of this. I'm frightened."

As if to make sure what he had seen was indeed gone, the gentleman took a step toward us, leaned our way and peered yet more deeply. We readied ourselves, though for what I'm sure we did not know.

"No more, I say!" She received no response. "Arthur!"

The gentleman turned, distracted by his wife's call, which afforded Holmes and me the opportunity to escape his further scrutiny by scurrying beside an oak filing cabinet. A stroke of good fortune, for when the good woman marched to the window and pulled open the draperies, flooding the room with the late-afternoon light, we were sufficiently concealed that neither she nor her husband noticed us. From that vantage point we were able to see and hear what was taking place.

What we saw was what appeared to be a study, decorated in what I would call well-ordered clutter, similar to the state of Holmes's quarters—and formerly mine as well—in Mrs. Hudson's domicile at 221B Baker Street. A summary glance revealed that the room contained several bookcases, one of them fronted by glass doors, the filing cabinet beside which we crouched, a desk and leather-backed desk chair, a deep-green carpet, and a fireplace on whose mantel were arrayed a variety of items. Near the doorway to the rest of the house was a chair, a small table, and an umbrella stand. On the walls were several paintings and drawings, a number of period firearms and swords, a large street map of London, and a calendar showing October 1893. Prominent in the centre of the room stood the round table at which the gentleman—for ease of narration, I will take the liberty of calling him Arthur, inasmuch as that appeared to be his name—and the two ladies had been sitting. On it sat a brass candlestick holding the burning candle, and a small framed photograph. Around it were three chairs, pushed back. Arthur's wife—for the same purpose, I will take the greater liberty of calling her Touie— proceeded now to this table and blew out the candle.

"Thank you, Madame Eneri," Touie said. "Thank you for trying, but…" She let the sentence die, its intent obvious. "We'll see you out." As she steered Madame Eneri and her husband towards the door, the latter, as if pulled, turned back to the room. "Arthur," she implored, "no!"

"Mrs. Doyle," said Madame Eneri, "if I may. A moment." She indicated the gentleman.

Touie hesitated briefly. "Yes, of course. I'll bring your coat. You had … was it an Ulster?"

"Yes, an Ulster. I fancy an Ulster. Grey."

Holmes and I glanced at each other in surprise. A woman wearing an Ulster? I did say exotic, did I not?

Touie left the room. Madame Eneri turned to the gentleman in time to see him pick up the walking stick and examine it closely. On his face, I read uncertainty. At this, Madame Eneri smiled and was about to say something, when Touie entered with her coat.

"Is this it, Madame?" she asked.

"Yes. Thank you."

"It's the very replica of Arthur's. I wasn't certain I had the right one." She turned to her husband, who at the moment was peering at the spot where we had appeared to him. "Madame Eneri is leaving, dear."

"Ah … ah, yes, of course." He put the walking stick down and took Madame Eneri's coat. "Terribly sorry, Madame. It was such a shock, seeing … seeing…"

"What?" his wife asked.

"Nothing, Touie. Nothing."

As he helped Madame Eneri into her wrap, Arthur paused to look at it. "Yes, Madame. Could be my Ulster. Identical." He followed the two ladies out, leaving me once again with the impression that I had seen this woman before.

Holmes and I held still a few seconds, relieved to see them gone. Just as we were about to step into the room proper, however, we heard Madame Eneri's voice. "No, don't trouble yourself, I can fetch them. I left them on the table, I believe. I'm blind without them."

We stepped back beside the filing cabinet just as Madame Eneri rushed into the room. She looked about as if searching for something. At last, she spied a small china figurine on a shelf behind the desk. She turned it over, and, verifying that it was hollow, took from her pocket the necklace and pendant. She held it out at arm's length, the ornament dangling, and made a slow turn in place. When, in her circling, she faced the spot where Holmes and I had first materialized to the gentleman—adjacent to where we now crouched in hiding—she paused and swung the ornament three times in our direction. Then she completed the circle, bestowed a kiss on the charm, and placed it inside the figurine, which she returned to its place on the shelf. Apparently satisfied with her efforts, she took a pair of eyeglasses from her reticule and put them on.

"Yes, here they are, Madame," she called to the next room, "on the table where I left them. And now here they are, safely on my nose, where they belong." She started from the room—"Yes, quite blind without them"—then turned in the doorway to take a last satisfied look, and at once, was gone. "So sorry to have caused you any…" Her voice receded as she went.

"I say, Holmes," I whispered, stepping out from our cover, "the eyeglasses. Did you ever see such—?"

"Brazenness? Indeed, yes." He came out into the room, "It is not only men who are capable of cunning. You remember, I assume, our unfortunate little adventure of the compromising letters we were to retrieve for—"

Suddenly, we heard someone coming. Again we scrambled to our hiding place, just as the gentleman of the house—Arthur—appeared in the doorway. From there, he scanned the room, then cautiously insinuated himself into it as if poised for what might be lurking. He edged over to the round table, lit the candle, then closed the draperies, recreating the room's earlier darkened state. Now he eased himself towards the corner in which he had seen—or thought he had seen—"them." He stared there now. As before, we held our breaths. After several long seconds, he shook his head, obviously disappointed. He uttered a grunt of dissatisfaction, then went to his desk, and with a furtive glance at the door drew from under a pile of papers a green manila folder. He opened it and stood looking down on its contents. He appeared deeply agitated.

Now he examined the walking stick where it stood against the wall. As did I, to my horror. I pointed it out to Holmes.

"There it is," Arthur said, muttering to himself. "Then … *did* I see…? Did I somehow … actually see them?" He looked around the room, clearly bewildered. "*Is* it his?" Again he leaned in and studied the stick, but now seemed reluctant to touch it.

"Why are you in the dark, Arthur?"

"A-h-h!!"

In the doorway stood his wife. "Sorry, dear. Didn't mean to startle you."

"I … How long have you been there?"

"How long have I…? Well, not long enough to see whatever it was you… What was it?"

"What was what?"

"What you saw. Or thought you saw. Or were trying to see again."

"I saw nothing. Just the shadows in there." He waved vaguely in our direction. His wife took a step that way. As she did so, Doyle moved as if to shield the desk from her view, or specifically the green folder, which he pulled in behind his back. She, however, wanted only to peer into the darkened corner—or might I now refer to it as "our" corner?

Much to our relief, she saw nothing and turned back to her husband. "As you say then, Arthur. But I don't know why you wanted to hold the sitting in this room anyway. The table, the extra chairs… The drawing room would have been preferable, don't you think?" As she said this, she took the framed photograph from the table and carried it across the room.

"Perhaps you're right, Touie. But I felt that here, my study, would be more … congenial to my purpose." He indicated the photograph. "Father." As Touie occupied herself rehanging the photograph in its spot on the wall, Arthur attempted to slide the green folder back under the pile of papers.

"He is utterly determined," Holmes whispered, "that she not see the contents of that folder. Interesting, that."

Before the gentleman could complete the task, his wife went over to the walking stick. "And this. Why were you so—?"

"My dear, you really must not trouble yourself over this. You know what happens when you excite yourself."

She picked it up and started across the room. "Oh, Arthur, I'm only—" Just as she was about to put the walking stick into the umbrella stand, she was seized by a fit of coughing.

"You see?" Arthur hurried over and put his arm around her. "Why do you insist?" He took the stick from her. At once he stiffened, head pulling in a bit, as though to shield himself from something unseen. Unknown.

"What is it, Arthur?"

Arthur seemed not to hear. Cautiously, he raised his eyes and scanned the upper reaches of the room, as if divining a terrible space.

"Give me that." Touie snatched the walking stick from him. Immediately her husband relaxed. "Lie there," she said, and thrust the object into the umbrella stand, but no sooner had she done so than she bent down and perused it. "Arthur, is this not the stick you've used for—"

"No matter."

And then ensued the following conversation, which Holmes and I could only wonder at:

"I only ask," Touie said, "because lately you seem obsessed with those two."

"No matter, I say."

"You've been so distracted. Is it the journey?"

"The journey, of course. Not obsessed at all. On the contrary, dear." He faced his wife and took her hands. "Neglectful. Of you. I hold myself responsible for your—"

"Arthur, I won't hear it. Please."

"But now, Switzerland will restore you. Complete rest."

"And your work?"

"I will simply go on with it there. Fewer distractions, in fact. Set your mind at ease. Trust me."

He leaned in to kiss her, from which—I confess—we did not avert our eyes. At the first touch of his lips, she laid her hand on his chest. "No more consulting Madame Eneri then? I'm still trembling from before. Your … apparition."

"That? Simply the figment of an overworked imagination, regrettably abetted by the heightened atmosphere of Madame Eneri's presence. An overworked imagination, moreover, which at the moment I should apply to the matter at hand." He completed the kiss, then broke away and returned to his desk.

"Are you going to work now, dear?"

"Yes, I think I might. I'm fairly desperate to finish this off." With that he sat down at the desk and resolutely slapped both hands on its surface, an obvious signal that he was poised for work and eager to get at it. Waiting for her to leave.

She stayed.

"You'll want light, no?" She went to the French windows and opened the draperies. In poured the gold-red of sunset, illuminating the room in its warm glow. And something besides. Standing in full view of the couple, having heedlessly let ourselves drift away from our cover, were Holmes and myself. Alarmed at our sudden exposure, we sidled over to the draperies as quickly as we dared and tucked ourselves into their harbouring folds. We saw no indication from Touie or Arthur of having noticed us. He, in fact, was at that moment attempting to conceal the green folder under his spread hands. In vain. As Touie came from the window, she glanced over his shoulder. "'*The Final Problem*,'" she read. "What is this, my dear?"

"It's nothing. Just a … a…"

"Story?"

"It is nothing. Why trouble yourself about it?"

"You've never minded before."

"But now I'm concerned about *you*. You should be resting."

As if to demonstrate how wrong he was, she went to one of the chairs that stood away from the round table and carried it the foot or so back to its proper spot, during which time Arthur seized the opportunity to slide the folder back under the pile of papers. His wife proceeded to the second chair, but as she lifted it, she was gripped by another fit of coughing. He rushed to her.

"There. Am I right?" From his desk he took a vial of medicine. "Here, at once, I want you to try a bit of this, my dear. Something new I've made up, to quiet the symptoms." She uncorked the vial and sniffed its contents, immediately jerking her head back. "Ah," he said, "must be effective. Correct dosage still to be determined, of course. Just a few more days, until we are safely away from this country. Come. We'll need water." He started out of the room.

"Arthur, I'd just as soon forego this for now. I'm sure I'll…" But he was gone. She put the vial on the desk and hurried after him. This time, Holmes and I let a half-minute go by before we felt it safe to emerge from the draperies.

"What do you make of that, Watson?"

"Your guess is as good as mine."

"I never guess. Let us, however, observe. First, the room. The curtains fully drawn in late afternoon. A single candle on a round table, which judging from the placement of the other furniture is but a temporary visitor to this space. I believe the lady alluded to that fact. Three chairs equally distanced around the table, all pushed back more than necessary. All three persons rose quickly, as we saw. Evidently one of them—or perhaps all—was surprised in the midst of some enterprise. You recall hearing the gentleman shout 'There! There!'"

"I do."

Holmes ventured over to the table, taking from his pocket his magnifying glass, which he applied to various areas of the cloth. "Interesting."

"What is it, Holmes?"

"From what I can detect, only two persons sat here. Yet, as you see, three chairs."

He debated that a moment, then nodded very slowly, a gesture which I knew indicated *"meaning yet to be determined … which it will be."*

"Whatever," Holmes continued, "at least two of them, one male, one female, sat at this table with their fingers pressed down. A meeting of sorts. Curious."

"A conspiracy?"

"Fingers pressed down."

Holmes saw my puzzlement.

"Concentration, Watson."

"I'm doing my best."

"As ever, but I refer to those who recently sat here, their fingers pressed hard to the table. *Why* were their fingers pressed hard to the table?"

"Ah! Because *they* were concentrating."

"And why do persons gather around a table, press their fingers to it, and concentrate?"

"A … séance?"

"There *are* those who believe in such proceedings." Holmes's distaste was obvious.

"A séance … just concluded."

"Watson, you are in rare form today. Save for one detail. As we seem to have observed, a séance just *abruptly* concluded."

"With only two persons?"

"So the evidence tells us. But we know three were here. A point of interest, no?"

"And you think they actually saw something?"

"You know as well as I there is nothing to see at these gatherings except charlatanism at its most rampant. The question is: what did they—ah, let me correct that. Not the ladies. From what we've observed, they saw nothing. The gentleman, rather. What did he *think* he saw, that caused such alarm?"

"Was it not us, Holmes? He appeared to point in our direction."

"Indeed he did. But, let us determine." Holmes's eye fell on the vial of medicine, where Touie had left it on the desk. "Ah, yes. This." He picked it up, and seeing no label, uncorked it and sniffed. His face screwed up at the smell.

"Ah," I said, "must be effective. May I?"

Holmes handed me the vial. I sniffed the contents and had the same reaction. "Not anything I recognize. Very new, whatever it is."

"New and worrisome. I like this not." From his pocket, Holmes—ever prepared to gather evidence—took an empty vial, poured a few drops of the medicine into it, and re-corked both. He returned his vial to his pocket—"We'll examine this back at 221B"—and the other to the desk top. "Let us, meanwhile, review what we have observed: a wife in obvious distress; a husband choosing her medicinal treatment. You heard. A 'new' medicine. 'Correct dosage to be determined.' The wife resistant. Does she suspect something? Same husband taking her abroad, and same husband obsessed—you heard her—obsessed with thoughts of 'those two.' What two?"

"Impossible to say, at this point."

"And then, did you mark his words? 'Safely away from this country?' Away, perhaps, from the arm of English law?"

"Perhaps. But one mustn't jump to conclusions."

"I never jump to conclusions. But I repeat: 'safely away from this country.'"

"That did sound ominous, I admit. But first..." I went to the umbrella stand and extracted the walking stick. "Glad to have this again. I don't mind telling you, Holmes, all the time she was holding it, I was in absolute—"

"What are you on about, my good fellow? *There's* your walking stick, precisely where you left it." Holmes pointed to our corner.

There, indeed, was my walking stick. I looked at the one in my hand, then retrieved my own. My eyes went from one to the other.

I held up the one that was truly mine. "Holmes, this walking stick was carved for me years ago, during my service in Afghanistan. By a native villager. I watched him do it. Watched it *being carved*. It is one of a kind." I held up the other. "Yet this is the identical object. How can that be?"

Holmes waved a periodical he'd been examining. "Elementary. *The Strand*. The man has obviously read some of your published accounts of my modest endeavours."

"They *are* quite popular."

"And has obtained a walking stick not unlike yours."

"*Identical*, Holmes."

"The explanation still holds." By now Holmes was perusing the bookshelves. "From the look of things, he's a medical man."

"We have something in common, he and I."

"You concoct experimental potions for your wife?"

"My Mary has never been ill a day since we met."

"Your salubrious influence, old man." At the desk, Holmes waved some stamped papers he'd been perusing. "And are you in the habit of purchasing one-way tickets for you and your Mary on the *Continental Express* from Victoria Station, connecting with the Channel boat to France, and then with a private railway carriage to Switzerland?"

"Holmes, ought we to be—?"

"Of course we oughtn't. But we have come to this place. Where a crime is pending? Recall his words, Watson: 'Desperate to finish this off.' Finish what off? Just who is this doctor?"

Holmes opened the covers of several books on the desk. "No name." He browsed among some papers there. "Is there no correspondence? Wait, the green folder, which he took some pains to conceal from his wife. There was a mild dispute over it." Holmes lifted the pile of papers and drew out the file. He opened it, leaned in and read. "'*The Final Problem*.'"

"Hello, what's this?" I said. On a side-table by the French doors lay a somewhat battered violin case. "It looks exactly like yours." I opened it. Inside lay an old, somewhat-worn, violin. "The violin as well, Holmes."

"How came this here?" Holmes's eyes were fixed on the instrument, his face now betraying deep and serious bafflement.

"Is it actually yours?"

"Obviously not," he answered. "But an exact replica, marks and all." Holmes studied the violin. "The ultimate test." He took it from its case and placed it under his chin. "Feels right." He took the bow from the case and lifted it to play.

"No, Holmes!" I raised my hand, then indicated the rest of the house.

"Ah, quite right." He lowered the violin. "The sudden rush to the familiar. Thank you, old man." He studied the instrument further, then with a puzzled look returned it to its case. "But I repeat: How came it here? Watson, there is strange work afoot."

"For that matter, Holmes, how came *we* here?"

"How…?" Holmes stared at me, struck by the question. "How…?"

Suddenly from the next room, we heard "Come, my dear. We seem to have left it in my study."

"Quickly!" Holmes stuffed the green folder back under the pile of papers. He gestured me to the draperies, then—"A draft"—blew out the candle and, closing the draperies as best he could, joined me behind them. At that moment the gentleman of the house, carrying a glass of water, entered the room, followed by his wife.

"Oh, the candle's blown out," he said. "Must be a draft somewhere." He pulled the draperies open. As he did so, Holmes and I sidestepped into the gather, in total concealment except, I noticed, for our protruding footwear. Through the uncovered windows now entered the last minutes of sunset, the first hint of dusk.

The gentleman retrieved the vial and uncorked it. "Now, dear, just a small dose of this, and hopefully…" He poured some of the medicine into the glass of water and held it out to her. The lady hesitated. I poked my head out, just enough to watch the proceedings.

Again he offered her the glass. "You must, my dear."

This time she took it, and—"I'm not sure which is worse, Arthur, the disease or the cure"—with a deep grimace drank it down. Almost at once, the good lady was wracked by another fit of coughing. She brought her handkerchief to her mouth and held it there until the attack subsided. She looked at it—"Oh, blessed God, not again"—and hurried from the room, followed by her husband.

Holmes and I waited what seemed a safe interval, then slid out from the curtains.

"That was cutting it rather fine," Holmes said. "Had they not been distracted by…"

"The cough," I said, absorbed in my thoughts.

"… they would be here still. While we…" Holmes pointed to our feet.

"That and the blood."

Holmes looked at me sharply. "The blood?"

"I saw it plainly, Holmes."

"Saw blood?"

"After she coughed. On her handkerchief."

We exchanged a horrified glance. "Consumption!"

"Switzerland," Holmes added. He pondered a moment. "That changes the complexion of things somewhat."

"So I have heard."

"I was referring, old man, to the complexion of the case. In any event, prudence dictates that, should they suddenly return…" He finished the thought by going to the French windows, opening them slightly, and indicating that this would be our escape route. "If necessary." He returned to the desk. "Would you be good enough, Watson, to keep an eye out?"

"Of course." I posted myself at the door.

"While I attend to this." Holmes slid the green folder from the pile of papers, opened it, and read. "'*The Final Problem. Reichenbach Falls.*'" He pondered. "Yes, of course." He settled himself at the desk. "Hearken to this, Watson. '*It is, indeed, a fearful place. The torrent, swollen by the melting snow, plunges into a tremendous abyss … an immense chasm … of incalculable depth.*' Rather stylish, if a bit over-done. Does this doctor fancy himself a writer?" Holmes skimmed ahead. "And this: '*The long sweep of green water roaring forever down, and the thick flickering curtain of spray hissing forever upward, turn a man giddy with their constant whirl and clamour.*' Or a woman?" Holmes looked at the doorway through which the couple had just departed.

He skimmed ahead. "What is *this*? '*The man pervades London, yet no one has heard of him. That's what puts him on a pinnacle in the records of crime.*'" Holmes pondered. "An accomplice?" And returned to the page. "'*He is the Napoleon of crime*'—Napoleon of crime?—'*a genius, a philosopher, an abstract thinker.*'" Holmes pondered again, obviously perplexed, obviously impressed. He skipped to the bottom of the page. "Good heavens, Watson, hearken to *this*: '*He is … Holmes's intellectual equal in every way.*'"

"Who is?!" I demanded.

"Who indeed? A…"—Holmes turned the page—"'*Professor James Moriarty.*'"

Immediately his hand went to his head. He knit his brows and held still, clearly waiting for the moment to pass.

"What is it, Holmes?"

"Nothing. A momentary dizziness."

"Now that you mention it, I felt a bit light-headed myself."

"The result, no doubt, of being witness to this man's scheming. I fear the matter is worse than I thought."

"He not only plots against the poor woman, but he writes it all down."

"Including the name of his evil accomplice: this Professor … Professor…" Holmes appeared to struggle with the name but finally managed to blurt it out: "James Moriarty. 'Pervades London, yet no one has heard of him.' Certainly I have not."

"Note that our doctor-writer has mentioned your name."

"Indeed. 'Holmes's intellectual equal.' We shall see about that. But first, the doctor. Who is he? *Is* he poisoning his wife? Why? How do we stop him? For that, we must change our method. The analytic will not do here. Not enough facts from which to deduce. No. We must turn to the synthetic method."

"The synthetic?"

"In which we synthesize a theory from the few facts we do have. Then, all subsequent evidence can be matched to that theory, which will either stand or fall, or be modified. So, what do we know at this juncture?"

"What was that about some waterfall?"

"Undoubtedly the reason for their impending departure to Switzerland. The Reichenbach Falls are one of the steepest cataracts in Europe. Could it be that he intends to lure his wife there, on pretext of a cure for her poisoned, weakened condition, where with the aid of this 'Napoleon of crime,' he will…?" Holmes made an over-the-edge gesture.

"Horrid!"

"Only if we do not foil him." Holmes closed the folder. "Search every corner of this room. There must be more."

We set about the task. Holmes started with the desk drawers, I with the room proper, but after a few moments I stopped. "Holmes? What exactly are we looking for?"

"Evidence. Any clue about this man. He's a medical colleague, Watson. See what you can find on that score. As we have observed, the man seems obsessed with me. Apparently he reads your published accounts of my adventures, then imitates your description of articles in my rooms at 221B Baker Street. My violin, as we have seen. You should be flattered."

"Hardly. It's you he's imitating."

"As revealed by you, my friend. But we stray. Search on."

We resumed our efforts, Holmes now at one of the bookcases, I examining the items on the wall. Suddenly I turned to my companion. "Holmes?"

"Yes?"

"I've never described your violin."

"I beg your pardon?"

"In all I've written about your exploits, I have only mentioned your violin. I have never actually described it."

We looked at each other blankly.

"Your walking stick?" Holmes's tone revealed more than a passing interest in the answer.

"Never described that either. This is inexplicable."

"*Nothing* is inexplicable. Let us reason. We have here a country doctor who records his notes in literary fashion. Is it endemic to your profession? And what is most striking, though I confess compositional analysis is not my forte"—Holmes opened the green folder—"his writing style seems remarkably similar to your own, though obviously not up to your level, old man. This time you, and you alone, should be flattered."

"Thank you, my friend."

"But whereas you have used your literary gifts to chronicle my humble pursuits, our gentleman"—Holmes held up the folder—"appears to be chronicling his own wife's less than humble demise. A dodge? The good lady herself seems to suspect he's up to something.

This case, Watson, is not without its points of interest." Holmes's face bore the hint of a smile.

"It couldn't merely be a story he's trying to write?"

Holmes brandished the papers he'd picked up earlier. "These tickets to Switzerland are no fiction. So, let us defer the one line of inquiry, and pursue the other. We have here—"

At that moment, the lady of the house—she who was called Touie—burst into the room. She glanced behind her, allowing Holmes and me not enough time to leave through the French windows but just enough to conceal ourselves within the room, Holmes this time by a tall bookcase and I once again by the oak filing cabinet. The lady carried an empty cardboard box, which she set down on a small table close by. Her proximity to our hiding places might well have allowed her to see Holmes and myself, but amazingly she did not. She went immediately to the filing cabinet, so distressingly close to me in my half-crouched position that I feared to breathe. She opened one of its drawers and extracted several folders, which she put into the box. That was when she noticed the green folder, on her husband's desk where Holmes had left it. She went to it eagerly. Holmes and I ventured to peek out.

She leaned over it, flipping and scanning the pages, then slipped into the desk chair and immersed herself in the writing. After a few seconds, she raised her head, pensive. "'The Final Problem,'" she murmured. On her face I saw deep concern. She returned to the page. "'*Reichenbach Falls.*'" Again she looked up. "Isn't that in Switzerland?" She read. "'*Rid of this burden at last.*'" She pondered, then scanned to another page. "'*…make certain that any attempt at recovering the body will be absolutely hopeless.*'" She scanned again. "'*The end must be utterly final.*'" She considered the words, which were as much a discovery for Holmes and myself as they were for her. "Whose end, my dear? Whose body?" She went back to the first page. "What '*burden?*' What are you planning, Arthur? Pray God it is not as I fear."

"Touie? Touie?"

The good lady closed the folder and hurriedly returned to the filing cabinet, where just as her husband burst into the room, she began a show of calmly taking out files and placing them in the box. Holmes and I, with no time to relocate—all this occurred in a matter of seconds—could only attempt, or rather hope, to shrink in place.

"Ah, there you are, my dear. What are you up to?"

"Just getting a start on your files."

"I can do that."

"Arthur, we've only three days left."

"I know, but I do not want you exerting yourself."

"It's no exertion." As if by way of proof, she demonstrated removing a file from the drawer and deftly transferring it to the box, ending the operation by gracing her husband with a disarming smile. He, however, was not to be disarmed. He stood by the open doorway, stolid, arms folded across his chest, the slight lean of his stance beckoning her to walk past him, no protest allowed, and out of the room. Instead, he heard "Arthur, weren't you going to work this evening?"

"I'd intended to, yes."

"Well, I enjoy being with you. So, you sit and do what you must, and I'll do the same over here."

Arthur hesitated, but seeing that his wife was determined to remain, uttered a resigned sigh and went to his desk. There before him was the green folder. After what appeared to be some moments of internal debate—had he not left it under the pile of papers?—and a long sceptical look at Madame, he gave his head a terse shake and lowered himself into his desk chair. He opened the folder, read a bit of what was there, then took up his pen. But he seemed unable to write. He glanced at his wife intent on her task, and sat resolutely still.

"How is it progressing?" she asked.

"Mmm, progressing." He saw her waiting for more. "Just … notes. Bits and snatches."

"Of…?"

He shrugged, as if to dismiss the possibility it could be anything important. The lady waited a few moments, then returned to the files. The doctor returned to the folder, but again her presence distracted him. He put down his pen, closed the folder, and slid it under the pile of papers. He rose. "Well, I think that's enough for today."

"But you haven't done anything."

"Can't concentrate. Anyway, close to dinner time. Come." He started out of the room. She held back. "My dear?" He offered his arm.

"I think I'll continue here a bit longer, Arthur. I'll join you in a few minutes."

This was obviously not what the gentleman had expected and was quite definitely not what he had in mind. Under no condition was he going to leave her alone here. He waited an awkward few seconds, then gently took from her hands the files she was holding, returned them to the file drawer and closed it. "You know the rules, my dear. No physical activity without me in attendance. Come. Dinner waits."

"Still time, Arthur."

"For a bit of sherry then." Again he held out his arm. Seeing no alternative, she put her arm in his, and with a last glance at the desk, allowed herself to be escorted from the room.

At once, Holmes and I emerged from the draperies. "Watson, did you notice the manner in which our gentleman—"

"I'll join you in a moment, my dear," came the doctor's voice. "I've forgotten something," followed at once by the doctor himself. There was no time for Holmes and me to take cover. All we could do was flatten ourselves against the wall and hold ourselves motionless, albeit in plain sight. The gentleman went straight to his desk, extracted the green folder, and transferred it to the top drawer, which he then locked. "Here I am, my dear!" he called as he left the room.

Holmes and I unstuck ourselves from the wall.

"I cannot believe he didn't see us."

"Oh, I can," Holmes replied. "Our doctor obviously has excellent powers of concentration. When one is intent on an objective, or in this case an object, one frequently sees nothing but *it*. That incriminating folder."

"Now locked away, unfortunately."

"Oh, that will present no problem," Holmes produced his penknife. "But we have new interests at the moment: those files. Why is he packing them away? Why will he not let his wife deal with them?"

"You heard him. Her health."

"And you heard her. No exertion in that. As indeed there is not. Might it be, Watson, that she is probing the man, trying to find out what he is about? Does she in fact suspect? And perhaps not realize that she is the intended victim?" Holmes gestured towards the door. "Have a lookout again, old man, though I doubt he'll return soon, now that he's locked away the evidence."

"And is enjoying his sherry and dinner."

"Well reasoned." Holmes went to the filing cabinet and began rummaging through the open drawer. "Hel-lo." He pulled out a file and read the title on its tab. "'*Silver Blaze*.'"

"'Silver Blaze?' 'Silver Blaze' my story? He's clipped it out?"

"He seems to have copied it out. It's in long-hand."

"Why would he do that?"

"Why, indeed?"

Holmes replaced the folder and pulled out another, considerably thicker than the first. He read its tab, then held it aloft.

"What is it, Holmes?" He gave me a wry smile. I hurried over. "Good Heavens. *A Study in Scarlet*. The entire novel?"

"It would appear so."

Despite my astonishment, I could not subdue a feeling of pride. "My first attempt at chronicling your exploits."

Holmes was already brandishing the next folder, also thick. "*The Sign of Four.*"

"My second," I said, my pleasure growing.

Holmes glanced through the two folders. "Considerable work, copying these two. Word for word, it appears. Extraordinary."

"Extraordinary, indeed," I said, looking through the file drawer. "It appears they are *all* here. Including"—I pulled out one of the folders and read its tab—"'*A Scandal in Bohemia.*'"

"Indeed," replied Holmes coldly.

"My first short piece after those two. Trying my hand at a more compressed form. I'm quite proud of the result, if I say so myself."

"You do."

Disregarding Holmes's cool response, I opened the folder and plunged in. "'*To Sherlock Holmes she is always*'—"

"... '*the woman,*'" he said, a less than joyous expression on his face.

"You do remember."

"Can I forget?"

"... '*the woman.*'" I read on. "'*I have seldom heard him mention her under any other name ... It was not that he felt any emotion akin to love for*—'"

"As you say." Again, the cool tone.

Undeterred—in fact, warming to the task—I browsed down. "'*And yet, there was but one woman to him, and that woman was the late Irene Adler.*' That is certainly as I remember it, Holmes. And"—I skipped to the last page—"as I ended it: '*And that was how ... the best plans of Mr. Sherlock Holmes were beaten by a woman's wit.*' Nice turn of phrase, that."

On I went. "'*He used to make merry over the cleverness of women, but I have not heard him do it of late. And when he speaks of Irene Adler … it is always under the honourable title of…*'"

"'…'the *woman*.'"

"Excellent." I patted the manuscript proudly and was about to close the folder when I noticed something curious. Something I had been staring at the whole time. "Holmes?"

"Yes?"

"Cast your eye on this." I held the open folder out to him. "Does it not strike you as peculiar? His handwriting. It's virtually identical to my own."

"That illegible scratching? Elementary, Watson. You're both doctors."

"Well, you may have your little joke, but … Hello, what's this?" I put down the folder I was holding and extracted the new find from the drawer. "Here's 'The Naval Treaty.' My latest. Good Heavens, the man is fast."

"As if compelled."

"What? To absorb my style by copying out my stories? Does he imagine he's actually writing them?"

"Perhaps the gentleman confuses penmanship with authorship."

I returned the folder to the drawer, when a new thought occurred. "Holmes?"

"Yes?"

"'The Naval Treaty.'"

"Yes. Your latest."

"It's more than that."

"More than that?"

"Holmes, 'The Naval Treaty' has not yet been published."

"What are you saying?"

"'The Naval Treaty' has not yet been—"

"Yes, yes, Watson, I heard that."

"I sent it off only last week. Yet here it is—"

"… complete in the man's own hand."

"My hand."

"As you say." Holmes pondered this new development. "*Is there a connection? Perhaps he's friends with Greenhough Smith.*"

"With my editor?" I shrugged at the possibility.

"Who may have shown it to him."

"For him to copy? I would hardly think so, Holmes."

Holmes dismissed the idea with a nod. He pondered further. "All right, then, the time has come." He took his penknife from his pocket and signalled me to station myself again at the door. A few deft pokes of the blade, a few turns, and he slid the top drawer open.

"That went easily," I said.

"Similar lock to the one at 221B. As is the desk."

He lifted out the green folder, sat down at the desk, and delved into it, skimming through until: "'*It had taken me an hour to come down. For all my efforts two more had passed before I found myself at the fall of Reichenbach once more.*'" He browsed further. "Ah, this may be it. '*There was his Alpenstock…*'"

"One of those mountain walking sticks."

"His … *Alpenstock?*" He read on, avidly. "… '*still leaning against the rock by which I had left him. But there was no sign of him.*'" He looked up. "'His? Him?' It would appear, Watson, that someone has indeed gone into the chasm, but … *is* it his wife?"

"He *wouldn't*. The dear lady is consumptive."

"We have seen worse, have we not?" Holmes read on. "'*He had remained on that three-foot path…*'" He struck the pages in frustration. "'He' again. Who?!" He read on. "…'*with sheer wall on one side and sheer drop on the other, until his*' … 'his' … '*enemy had overtaken him. The young Swiss who brought the note calling me away had gone too. He had probably been in the pay of…*'" Here Holmes hesitated and passed his hand across his eyes. "Oh, that name." He seemed unable to go on. He waited several seconds for the indisposition to pass, then re-addressed himself to the page. "…'*in the pay of…*'" Again he hesitated, seemingly unable to battle through the obstacle he was encountering.

I went to the desk and peered over his shoulder. "'*Moriarty.*'" I returned to my post.

Holmes let out a sharp escape of breath. "Thank you, Watson." He took a few moments, then continued reading. "…'*and had left the two men together.*' Do you hear, Watson? Men. Two." He read on. "'*And then what had happened? Who was to tell us what had happened then?*'" Holmes paused and thought.

"Is that all?"

"That is all. 'Two men.' What do you make of it, Watson?"

"I don't. It's not a story *I* wrote."

Holmes looked off, musing. "Not a story you wrote. Jottings, rather. Jottings for something to do with his 'final problem.' In a story, as you say. That you did not write. It all fits."

"It does? Ah, the analytic method again." Holmes gave no response. "The synthetic?"

"Quite right. The analytic is not working."

"I see. And what does the synthetic suggest?"

"That what we have here are notes—notes for what is not *yet* a story. And why, my friend?"

"Why, indeed," I said, more in bafflement than inquiry.

"Because it never will be a story."

"Never will…? I'm afraid you've lost me, old chap."

"Because it is *not* a story."

"So you have said."

"Notes, Watson, for what *looks* like a story but which in reality is something quite different."

"What are you saying, Holmes?"

"Notes disguised."

"Notes disguised?"

"As something other than what they are."

"What are they?"

"Plans. Plans for the murder. All his copying of your works is an elegant subterfuge—a somewhat laborious one, I admit, but have we not seen the criminal mind even more dogged than this? A subterfuge for his nefarious scheme, written out here in order to be communicated, undetected, to..." The name caught in his throat. Holmes gestured to me to say it.

" ...his fiendish Irish confederate."

"Yes, Watson. As we suspected. But the murder is not of his wife. There we were mistaken. She is not the one in danger."

"Except from that dreadful disease."

"But someone else is: a man, as yet unnamed. 'He ... Him ... His.'" Each word was accompanied by a sharp finger-jab to the green folder, as if to prod it into revealing the unknown identity.

"But, Holmes, clearly the doctor's purpose in going to Switzerland is to cure his wife of her consumption."

"Yes, too clearly."

"Too clearly?"

"Too clearly his purpose. Less clearly—to others, at least—his convenient cover."

"For what?"

"For the deed at Reichenbach Falls. A fearful place, Watson. Despite our doctor's inferior literary gifts, he describes it vividly. He has learned well ... at your elbow, shall we say?"

"His literary skills only, I assure you."

Holmes rose. "We must waste no time in warning the intended victim."

"But who is it?"

"Well may you ask. And who is this doctor? And who is his accomplice, this..."

" … Moriarty."

Holmes winced, but a moment later managed to wave it off. "To work. I am convinced this room holds the knowledge we seek. As is the lady. Did you note how she pretended to be removing the files when actually she was snooping at the desk?"

"Yes. I was surprised she could dissemble as well as that."

"Oh? Have you forgotten?" Holmes brandished the "A Scandal in Bohemia" folder, which I had left on the desk.

"Ah, yes. Irene Adler."

"That most dissembling woman. Even to the point of disguising herself in male attire."

"Indeed." I touched the folder affectionately. To me, it contained hallowed words, albeit in another's hand. "'A slim youth in an Ulster.'" I could not resist imitating her voice, just as I remembered it—with its slight upward lilt—and just as I had written it: "'Good night, Mr. Sherlock Holmes.'"

"All in the past, Watson. But it gives me an idea. We will set a trap. The doctor fancies himself a writer, does he? You, Watson, are the true writer here. A similar compositional style, a similar hand. I have need of all that."

"I stand ready."

"As ever. Sit." Holmes offered me the desk chair. "Take pen and paper. I want you to create fresh material for—or rather *by*—our good doctor here. First, a brief sentence to be added to this supposed story he is writing, but with an invented name for the intended victim."

I took a piece of paper from the pile, picked up the gentleman's pen, similar to my own, and set to write. "What name, Holmes?"

"Any name will do. Invent."

"Gladly. And second?"

"Second, on another sheet a few lines describing how Holmes and Watson, summoned one late afternoon to the home of a certain country doctor…"

"Still a mystery there, Holmes."

"As I said, old man, the case is not without its points of interest." Holmes pointed to the sheet of paper before me. "…summoned one late afternoon to the home of a certain country doctor, happen upon evidence that said doctor is planning a murder."

"What do you hope to accomplish by this, Holmes?"

"I must rattle this man, Watson, to see what he will reveal. To confirm our synthesized theory and lead us to the intended victim. Commence!"

I started to write, but after a half-minute lowered the pen. "Nothing's coming."

"Writer's block. All authors have it."

"I never have. It has always been effortless."

"Well, keep at it. It is crucial."

Again I addressed myself to the blank page, and Holmes to his search of the room. "Good Heavens!" he suddenly exclaimed. "Look at this, old man." Stuck to the mantel with a knife was a small pile of correspondence. Holmes pulled out the knife and held up the correspondence, the knife stuck through it.

"What? Your correspondence?! Here??"

"No, the good doctor's."

"Stuck to the mantel in exactly the same way as yours. How extraordinary."

Holmes regarded the knife and the envelopes it held, clearly struck by the likeness to his own method at 221B, and just as clearly puzzled by it. He read the top envelope. "Well, not so very far from home after all. Surrey, Watson."

"A stone's throw."

"South Norwood, to be exact."

"I shall use that."

"Use his name also. Doyle. Dr. A.C. Doyle."

"Doyle," I mused. "Doyle." I shook my head. "Never heard of him." And returned to my writing. Several times, however, I had to break off, again encountering great difficulty. In fits and stops, however, I managed to continue, so that a few minutes later I was able to announce: "Finished. Part the First. Have a look." I handed Holmes the sheet of paper.

"'*It is with a heavy heart,*'" he read, "'*that I take up my pen to write these the last words in which I shall ever record the singular gifts by which my friend Mr. Florian Beauregard was distinguished.*' Rather long getting to the victim, Watson, but it will serve the purpose, I think."

"I saw it as a possible introductory sentence to the purported story."

"Ah, I see. Very good."

"Do you like the name I invented? Florian Beauregard? It has a certain … jauntiness, don't you think?"

"The name is immaterial, old man, so long as it is not the one the doctor intends." Holmes placed the page on the desk, next to the green folder. "Let it reside there. Now, Watson, the other. I will in the meantime continue at my task."

I again set to work, though again with uncustomary difficulty putting words to paper. Holmes resumed his search, from time to time moving to the door to check for sounds of anyone coming. "If they should return before you have finished"—Holmes pointed to our hiding place in the draperies—"and be sure to take that with you. He must read it only in its completed state, and I, Hamlet observing Claudius, must see him do so."

He continued his tour of the room and came to a glass-fronted bookcase, whose doors he found locked. "Curious," he mused. At that moment, however, his eye was caught by another object over the fireplace. "Hello, what is this?" From the mantel he took an unframed photograph. "Cast your eye here, my friend." I stared at the photograph in amazement. "Yes, Watson. Your photograph of that American writer."

"Henry Ward Beecher. On the mantel at 221B."

"On the mantel *here*."

"But … Beecher gave that to me personally, years ago, when I was over there."

"Signed 'To A.C. Doyle'?"

I peered at the photo. "How is this possible? The photograph was one of a kind."

"You watched it being carved."

"Yes. No! I … I tell you, Holmes, this is inexplic—"

Holmes's warning finger stopped me. "Nothing is."

"Well, then how in the world can this be?"

"What did you say?"

"I asked, how in the world—"

"Stop!"

"What is it, Holmes?"

"What you said." Holmes lowered his eyes and covered his brow with his hand, a familiar pose when he was in deepest concentration. Finally, he looked up, shaking his head. "I have been feeling it for the past little while: We come upon these objects, we hear and see what occurs in this room, yet my thoughts go so far, so far, and no farther. It is like a barrier, an impenetrable wall I cannot get beyond." He clenched his fists in frustration. "WHERE AM I?"

"Easy, old chap. South Norwood."

"No. It is more than that. Let us … for Heaven's sake … let us reason."

He went around the room again, reviewing the items: the manuscript on the desk, the violin case, Doyle's files, the walking sticks, the knife-stuck envelopes, the Beecher photograph. He added up all the clues. "Nothing. Nothing! Why will my head not work today?!" His desperation visible, he turned to me. "Have you finished?"

"Almost." I perused what I'd written. "What would you think of a florid ending?"

"I would think better of an immediate ending. They may be back from dinner at any moment. And the moment I hear them, I shall whisper 'someone is coming.'"

"Very good." I returned to my writing.

"Someone is coming," Holmes whispered.

"Got it, old chap. And the moment you do, I shall—"

"Then please do! Someone is *coming*! Have you—?"

"Finished." I rose at once and placed the paper among the others on the desk.

"Quickly, then." Holmes indicated the draperies. "And keep a sharp eye and ear. We'll soon find out what"—he stopped, then tilted his head as if tuned to something unseen—"in the world..." At once, he shook himself out of it, put the green folder back in the desk drawer, then joined me behind the gathered curtains, our shoes once again distressingly exposed, just as Madame Doyle—I am so relieved that I needn't use her given name anymore—entered.

She went straight to the desk, lit the desk lamp, and looked again for the green folder. Instead, she found my invented passages. She perused them avidly, then raised her head, on her face a mixture of puzzlement and distaste. "'Florian Beauregard?'" She looked at the page, her expression now changing to scepticism, and thence to suspicion. "No. No. A ruse." At that moment, she heard her husband approaching. She shuffled the new page among some others on the desk and hurried to the French windows, which of course brought her perilously close to us. She stood there, making a show of looking out, as Dr. Doyle entered the room. "Did you leave this open, Arthur?"

"Not I, dear."

"Ah, we are invaded by spirits." She closed the French windows.

"Hopefully the benevolent ones that just occupied the kitchen. An excellent dinner, my dear. Please tell cook. Speaking of which, you'll be pleased to know that I have engaged a first-rate person in Switzerland."

"One who knows all your favourite dishes?"

"I shall be the first to inform her."

"*I* shall."

"Mmm, so I fear. Because that is not the important thing." He put his arms around her. "What matters, Touie, is that once there, you rest and regain your strength. Which begins with not worrying about whether I am being served my favourite dishes."

"I shall try, dear, but old habits…" She kissed her husband on the cheek, went to the file cabinet and began removing files.

"… unfortunately die hard." He took the files from her hands.

"Arthur, I shall handle only one folder at a time. Go and do your work." She shooed him to the desk. As before, he held back. "I've lit the lamp, Arthur. Now go." He went. "Sit." He sat. "Work." She waited. Doyle took out his desk key and displayed it for her approval. She nodded. "You won't know I'm here."

Madame Doyle returned to the files, made a performance of taking out only one folder at a time, then, half-turning away, put on a show of disinterest in what he was doing. He watched her a few seconds, then with a sigh applied his key to the desk drawer. He was surprised to find it unlocked, and gave his wife a questioning look. She, demonstrably unaware of his actions, went on transferring folders from file cabinet to box, occasionally leaving on the table two or three that perhaps interested her particularly.

"Did you say all of these, dear?"

"Every last one," Doyle answered, "into permanent storage." He removed the green folder from the drawer. "And I do mean last, when this one is done."

He opened the folder, mindful that she might be watching. As he bent to work, she sidled up behind him, trying to peek over his shoulder. At that moment, Doyle noticed the file containing "A Scandal in Bohemia," which I, in my haste to reach the drapery folds, had left on the desk. "What's this, my dear? Did you miss this one?"

"Which? Oh, 'A Scandal in Bohemia.'"

"My first short piece after the two novels. Trying my hand at a more compressed form. I'm quite proud of the result, if I say so myself."

My own words! I was so flabbergasted that I almost blurted out my amazement.

"Irene Adler," Madame Doyle said.

"Irene Adler, indeed. *The* woman. Holmes's match in every way."

Behind the curtains, I saw Holmes start.

"I often wondered," Doyle continued, "what would have happened had they become, shall we say, romantically involved."

I saw Holmes wince.

"Anyway," Doyle went on, "too late now. She stays where she is." Nevertheless, he opened the folder. "Ah, yes. Remember? The King of Bohemia calls her '*the well-known adventuress Irene Adler.*' And Holmes, smart fellow, says to the king"—here, to my utter astonishment, Dr. Doyle duplicated Holmes's voice and inflection perfectly—"'*…Your Majesty, as I understand, became entangled with this young person, wrote her some compromising letters, and is now desirous of getting those letters back.*'"

I glanced at Holmes and saw that he, too, was amazed to hear his own words from back then, exactly as he had said them. With each word, I saw his increasing discomfort, much as if a voodoo doll of himself were being jabbed incessantly.

"And then," Madame said, warming to the narrative, "Holmes, smart fellow, concocts a ruse to get the letters back."

"And fails. Remember? And to add insult to injury, that evening, as he and Watson, unsuccessful, return to his lodgings"—Doyle browsed in the manuscript—"Ah, here it is. '*We had reached Baker Street and had stopped at the door. He was searching his pockets for the key when someone passing said: "Good night, Mister Sherlock Holmes." There were several people on the pavement at the time, but the greeting appeared to come from a slim youth in an Ulster who had hurried by. "I've heard that voice before," said Holmes, staring down the dimly lit street. "Now, I wonder who the deuce that could have been."*'"

As Doyle quoted Holmes's words, I saw Holmes mouth them in unison.

"I remember," Madame Doyle said. "The young man…"

"Young woman."

"Yes, of course. It was…"

"… as it turns out…"

"… Irene Adler herself," they said together.

"In male guise," Doyle added. "She had seen through Holmes's ruse, worked out the whole business, and even followed him and Watson from her house to 221B Baker Street."

Holmes's expression was grim.

"Just to play this little joke on him," Madame Doyle said with glee.

"'Good night, Mister Sherlock Holmes.'" Doyle looked at his wife, his enjoyment evident. "Oh, the wonderful, audacious lady. Remember how Watson, the old reprobate, had described her?" He browsed back. "Ah, here it is. '*Irene Adler … had hurried up the steps; but she stood at the top with her superb figure outlined against the lights of the hall…*' Nice turn of phrase, that. As is"—he skimmed ahead joyfully—"'*she was a lovely woman, with a face that a man might die for.*' And, Touie, a mind that Holmes might have embraced." Doyle shook his head sadly. "And now, I must replace her consummate intelligence, beauty, and daring with this fiend Moriarty."

Holmes, beside me, bent over in absolute pain. I, also, truth be told, felt a pronounced discomfort.

"With *whom*, Arthur?"

A look of panic crossed Doyle's face. "Oh, no one, my dear, just a … no matter." He handed his wife the "A Scandal in Bohemia" file—"Here you are, my dear. For your box."—then turned at once to the papers on the desk. Which was when he saw the first of my efforts. "What is this?"

I brightened in anticipation.

He leaned in. "'*It is with a heavy heart that I take up my pen to write these the last words in which I shall ever record the singular gifts by which my friend Mr. Florian Beauregard was distinguished.*' Florian Beauregard?!! Who the deuce is that? And how comes this here?" He looked at the good lady his wife with more than a trace of suspicion. "Touie, do you know anything about this?"

She had already taken the page and was examining it. "No, Arthur, it appears you wrote it. It's in your hand, is it not? But 'Florian Beauregard?' What a ghastly name. Wherever did you find it?"

"I didn't. Nor any of this. I think. I assume. Lately, my…" He touched his head and gave it a slight shake, then perused the paper, frowning. "*Did* I write that? It is certainly in my hand. And in my style. Actually, it's not too bad. In fact, it's quite good."

I swelled at the compliment.

"In fact," Doyle continued, "might it not serve as the opening sentence for this story I'm working on? Aside from that hideous name, of course. 'Florian Beauregard,' indeed." He gave a slight shudder. "I *have* been preoccupied."

"What should the name be, Arthur?"

"Oh … nothing. Just not that. Absurd."

"Why not write in the proper name, then?"

She leaned in to watch him do it, as did Holmes and myself—as much as we dared.

"No hurry," Doyle said.

Holmes shot me a frustrated look. Madame Doyle, likewise upset, could only return to the file cabinet and her task of transferring folders into the cardboard box. Occasionally, one caught her attention and she stopped to browse in it.

As Doyle set himself to write, his eye fell on my second piece. "Hello, what is *this*? '*Whereas, over the years, mysterious disappearances have engendered many of the fruitful investigations by my friend Mr. Sherlock Holmes and myself, Dr. John Watson, nothing can explain our mysterious appearance one late afternoon in the South Norwood home of a certain Dr. A. C. Doyle.*' What??!! '*In looking for some clue to why we had been summoned there, we happened upon evidence of something urgent and unsettling: a murder about to be committed by that same Dr. Doyle. Victim: one Florian Beauregard. Clearly, Dr. Doyle was a man to be reckoned with most seriously, a man who would spare no effort to achieve his dark ends.*'"

Doyle's jaw dropped, his body went slack, as, dumbstruck, he stared at the passage. Seeing the marvellous effect my words had on him, I was, I must confess, as thrilled as a schoolboy who has just come top in Composition.

The gentleman read the passage over and over, obviously trying to probe its words, its meaning, its origin. At last he looked up, a knowing smile on his face.

"Tou...ie."

"Yes, dear."

"You are carrying things too far."

"Only from here to the table. It's not heavy, Arthur. I promise you I'm not exerting myself."

"I am not referring to that." He held up the page. "This."

"A new story, Arthur? Fascinating premise. But I thought you disliked that Florian Whatever name."

Doyle gave his wife an indulgent look. "Stop dissembling, dear. It's unlike you to joke in this manner."

"I?"

"You. Did you not write this, and leave it here for me to find?"

"No more than the other piece."

The look he gave his wife this time was somewhat less indulgent. "Touie, you are"—her own expression, completely artless, stopped him—"telling the truth."

"When have I not, dear?"

"Who, then? Who wrote this?"

"A credible copy of your style, I must say. And of your hand. And it seems a wonderful idea for a story."

"Nevertheless. Has anyone been here today?"

"Only Madame Eneri. But she left long before dinner."

"And I've been here since. And I can swear this was not here till now. You've seen no one?"

"No one, Arthur."

"The French windows were open."

"Ah. As I said. Spirits."

Dr. Doyle again perused the passage. "*Did* I write this? Like"—he held up my first piece—"this other? But how did I come to…? And when? I couldn't have."

"Well, my dear, you *have* been acting strange lately. Have you not?"

"Simply nerves. Your illness, my dear. The coming voyage."

"And this afternoon?"

"This afternoon?"

"What … whom … did you see?"

"No one. I saw no one!"

"Arthur, what is going on? You are being accused of plotting a murder."

"You think I am capable of—?"

"I think no such thing. But there is, has been for some weeks now, something in the air. You have been erratic." She moved closer to the desk and leaned in, fingers touching the pages I had written. "Arthur, who is Florian Beauregard?"

"Stop tormenting me with that abomination. There is no such person! A fiction, even less real than—" He stopped as if a hand had suddenly clamped itself over his mouth.

"Than whom?" She waited. "Than *whom*, Arthur?" He gave no answer. "Arthur, you must tell me." Still nothing. "Arthur, I am your wife." He half turned away, shunning her gaze. "Arthur, this afternoon, at the table with Madame Eneri, *whom did you summon?*"

"I summoned no one! How could I? They were not on my mind at the time. I should not have seen them before me." Doyle sank in the desk chair, despair on his face. "It is worse than I thought."

"What is?"

"Oh, Touie. I'll show you."

He went to the glass-fronted bookcase. "It's all here, in a new poem." He took a key from his watch-fob, unlocked the door, and took out a leather-bound portfolio.

"I call it 'The Inner Room.'" He opened the portfolio—"First stanza"—and, his voice betraying great agitation, read:

> "*It is mine--the little chamber,*
> *Mine alone.*
> *I had it from my forbears*
> *Years agone.*
> *Yet within its walls I see*
> *A most motley company,*
> *And they one and all claim me*
> *As their own.*'"

Madame Doyle raised her hand slightly, stopping her husband as he was about to read on, allowing herself time to fathom what she'd heard. "I should think that a happy condition in one who writes."

"While writing, yes," Dr. Doyle replied. "But, the next stanza:

> '*There are others who are sitting,*
> *Grim as doom,*
> *In the dim ill-boding shadow*
> *Of my room.*
> *Darkling figures, stern or quaint,*
> *Now a savage, now a saint,*
> *Showing fitfully and faint*
> *Through the gloom.*'"

"What are you saying, Arthur?"

"I am saying that is exactly what occurred this afternoon. Frequently, Touie, while working, bringing to life my 'people,' I see them here in front of me. But this afternoon I was not working. I did not have them in mind. Yet, there they were. He. Showing through the gloom."

"'He?'"

"'*He!*' My obsession! This weight I must lift from my shoulders. This man I must remove forever from the face of the earth." He turned from her, quite agitated, and replaced the portfolio in the bookcase, which he then locked with a resolute turn of the key. He returned the key to his waistcoat pocket.

Madame laid her hand on her husband's arm. "What man? *What man*, Arthur? Arthur, you must tell me what is going on. This does sound like murder."

I could see from Dr. Doyle's expression that he was torn how to reply. And he could see from his wife's expression, earnest but determined, that it was no use holding out any longer. He went to the desk, sat, and opened the green folder. "As you surmised, my dear, a story. A final story. You don't mind a bit more?"

"I love when you read to me."

"I'm afraid you won't love this, my dear."

Madame sat down on one of the chairs at the round table, all attention. From our place of concealment Holmes and I, having devoured all we had heard so far with a mixture of compulsion, confusion, consternation, and alarm, strained to hear more.

"It's still incomplete," Doyle said. "Except for the ending." He turned to the last page, then looked at Madame—something between a concern and a caution— and read, "*A few words may suffice to tell the little that remains. An examination by experts leaves little doubt that a personal contest between the two men ended, as it could hardly fail to end in such a situation, in their reeling over, locked in each other's arms.*'"

"'Reeling over?'"

"Reichenbach Falls."

The good lady gasped. "What two men?!" she and Holmes exclaimed at the same moment.

Doyle ignored her question, and fortunately did not appear to have heard Holmes. Instead, he continued reading, as if fully determined to get it over with. "'*Any attempt at recovering the bodies was absolutely hopeless, and there, deep down in that dreadful cauldron of swirling water and seething foam, will lie for all time the most dangerous criminal and the foremost champion of the law of their generation.*'"

"Arthur, you don't mean … you *can't* mean…" Clearly, Madame could not complete the thought, much less the sentence.

"My newest find: Professor Moriarty."

"No. The other one."

"Evil. Remorseless. And brilliant. A necessary match for our persistent detective."

"'Our persistent'…? Then you do mean…?"

Behind the curtains, Holmes, who—in addition to the confusion and deep unease we both felt—had been showing signs of great distress from the moment Doyle began reading, was now struck by a sharp stab of pain at the mention of the name Moriarty.

By way of answer to his wife, Doyle flipped back a couple of pages, and read, "*'It had taken me an hour to come down.'*" He stopped and glanced at Madame. "'*Me*' being Watson, of course. Away from the falls."

At mention of my name, a shudder of dread coursed through me.

Doyle read on. "*'For all my efforts two more had passed before I found myself at the fall of Reichenbach once more. There was his Alpenstock...*" Doyle shook his head in dismay. "Clarity, man. Clarity." He crossed out a word and inserted its replacement. "'*There was*'"— he gave his wife a look of foreboding—"'*There was* Holmes's *Alpenstock, still leaning against the rock by which I had left him.*'"

"What?!!" cried Madame Doyle.

Holmes and I looked at each other, utterly aghast. Doyle, evidently liberated by the anticipated response from his wife, aimed his reading directly at her. "'*But there was no sign of him, and it was in vain that I shouted.*'"

Madame's hand went to her breast. "Are you saying, Arthur—tell me you are not—that it is … it is … that the intended victim is…"

Doyle picked up my first piece and waved it defiantly. "*Not* Florian Beauregard. But yes. That other.*" He went back to page one and read as if in confirmation: "'*It is with a heavy heart that I take up my pen to write these the last words…*'"

"No, Arthur!"

Holmes, though like myself struggling to make sense of the couple's conversation, nevertheless shook his head along with Madame, as vigorously as his increasingly debilitated state would allow.

"Yes, my dear," Doyle went on, "the 'two men.' Struggling. Then … both"—his hand described an over-the-edge flip—"into that chasm, and there's a finish to the whole business. To be completed this very evening."

Madame Doyle rose and faced her husband, confronting him with her whole devoted being. "Arthur, you cannot do this. Think of your readers. Thousands. *Hundreds* of thousands. We love him!"

"Touie, the man has had two novels and almost two dozen stories. Quite enough for anyone. He has taken my time from my more serious writing, he—"

"Think of your dear mother! *She* loves him. *I* love him! We need him!"

"He has taken my time from *you*! That must stop! You, Mother, Father—were he still here—and those many thousands, will simply have to accept it. Trust me, my dear. I shall do it delicately. No visible body. But the deed must be done. The deed *will* be done. For this"—he held up the piece I had written—"has demonstrated the depth of my captivity to this man."

Holmes was immediately bent over by what looked to be a splitting pain to his entire body, the earlier feeling of weakness now greatly magnified. He tried to keep to his feet, but finally staggered out from the curtains and into a chair near to us. He struggled for breath. I went to his aid, unmindful that we might now be completely visible. This time our luck ran out. Dr. Doyle was facing in our direction. Even while occupied with Holmes, I heard…

"In fact, at this very instant, Touie, I see him sitting right there, his doctor friend with him. It is unbearable." I saw Doyle make a gesture of rejection, a cry of utter disgust, and turn away from us. I can only say that I was flabbergasted and terrified by it all … and also, I must confess, more than a bit put out.

"My poor Arthur," said Madame, her attention totally on her husband, so that she, at least, was not looking in our direction.

"No, Touie. My decision is made. Our hero will depart this life. The moment has come for the final problem to be solved." I looked up to see Doyle again at his desk, again address himself to the manuscript before him. He bent over the page and scanned what was there, then took up the version I had written. "Yes, I do like this as an opening. Except, of course, for that name. *'It is with a heavy heart that I take up my pen to write these the last words in which I shall ever record the singular gifts by which my friend'*"—he crossed out the name I had written, and in a firm hand and bold voice substituted— "*'Mr. Sherlock Holmes … was distinguished.'*"

My own words being used to condemn Holmes! I was devastated by the utter horror of it. I shook my head and waved my hand to and fro, as if to wipe out the possibility.

"Yes, Touie," Doyle continued, "the perfect opening, for the perfect ending!"

He began writing furiously.

"No!" called Holmes as strongly as he was able. He rose from his chair, swaying, and lurched towards the doctor bent over the manuscript. As Holmes advanced on him, I, fearing for my friend's stability, advanced with him.

Doyle gave his head a violent shake. "No!" he shouted. "You no longer rule here!!" He held up a hand towards Holmes, as if to ward him off, while with the other he continued writing, as if driven by some demon. Touie, who had still taken no notice of Holmes and me, stared at her husband in alarm.

"Stop!" Holmes cried. "Do not…!"

Doyle clutched his head, forcibly ignoring Holmes's voice, and seemed to will his writing hand back to the page. Only with great effort now, as if pushing his pen through some viscous medium, did he manage to set down a few words on paper. Holmes, even in the midst of his incomprehension—as well as the baffling infirmity that was afflicting him—seemed to know that he simply had to stop Dr. Doyle from writing further. He tried frantically to reach Doyle's hand. At the same moment, Madame Doyle, alarmed by her husband's erratic behaviour, started towards the gentleman. Just as Holmes was about to seize Doyle's hand, the doctor made a powerful gesture to thrust him off. Thus rejected, Holmes turned as if slapped, and found himself face to face with Madame Doyle.

Again she exclaimed "Oh, Arthur!" and continued towards her husband quite as though Holmes were not right there in her path. Just as she appeared about to collide with him, Holmes stepped out of her way, and she, without breaking stride or giving Holmes so much as a glance, rushed past him. Utterly stunned by this, Holmes peered at his hands, touched his body, as if questioning their substantiality. His face was drained of all expression save uncomprehending terror, evidence of a mind reeling uncontrollably. A frozen moment elapsed, and then he sank to his knees. I rushed to him.

Doyle saw us. "You! And you! You still think to haunt me?! No more!" He flourished the manuscript. "Remember?" And in a mocking tone: "'Good night, Mr. Sherlock Holmes.'" Then, in glee, in triumph: "Good night, indeed. Rest in peace!"

With that, he turned from us and snatched up his pen. But suddenly he stopped, and, head barely lifted, scanned the room as if sensing a presence. Cautiously he looked up, to see a figure looming in the dim corner. It was a slim youth in a grey Ulster.

"You!" cried Doyle.

"You!" I cried.

The youth approached Holmes. Doyle was transfixed. I was stupefied.

"What is it, Arthur?" Madame Doyle said, fearful eyes only on her husband.

The youth stood over Holmes, looking down at him.

"They haunt me!" Doyle cried to his wife. "All of them! They haunt me even now!"

"Arthur, you are distraught. So much on your mind."

"Will I ever be free of them?"

"Come." She helped the unresisting doctor from his chair and guided him towards the door. "It's your nerves. And, is it not, a heavy, heavy load of guilt?"

"No more! Please, let us go. Pray God they will not follow."

They left the room. I murmured a prayer of thanks.

Holmes was showing signs of recovering. "What happened? He … was about to…" At that moment, he raised his eyes and saw standing over him the Ulster-clad youth. "Who … is that?" He squinted up at the figure. "Have I not seen you before?"

"Indeed you have. 'Good night, Mr. Sherlock Holmes.' For so it seems."

"I've heard that voice before."

"That also." The youth removed his cap. Down tumbled a woman's full head of hair.

Holmes stared in amazement. "*You* here. *The* woman."

"Irene Adler," I gasped, my own astonishment narrowing my voice to barely above a whisper.

"Whose help, Mr. Sherlock Holmes, you…"

"He was about to…" Holmes struggled to rise.

"… desperately need."

But could not.

"Feeling out of your element, Mr. Holmes?" Irene Adler said, looking down at him.

"She did not see me." Holmes looked at his hands. "*Did … not … see me*! I …am …"

"No longer 'in the world?'" Miss Adler said. "Shall we join forces, then?"

Holmes seemed to only half hear. "Join…?"

"Against those arrayed against you. Dr. Arthur Conan Doyle. And his creature-to-be, Professor Moriarty. What say you, Mr. Sherlock Holmes? Are you ready to cross that great barrier?"

Holmes looked at her blankly, as if trying in the midst of his distress to decipher her words, as if trying, in fact, to determine if they actually had come from her. Again a frozen, laboured moment, and my esteemed friend and colleague crumpled to the floor.

II

Ten minutes had passed, with Holmes lying where he fell, I in attendance. I had arranged him into a less contorted position than that into which he had dropped, and placed a small chair cushion under his head. Irene Adler was nowhere to be seen. She had obviously slipped out of the room for some reason while I was seeing to my colleague. At length, Holmes opened his eyes. He made an effort to get up.

"Steady, old man. Don't attempt to rise yet."

He laid back down and scanned the space above him. "Am I sunk so low?"

"Not exactly, old fellow. You fainted."

"Fainted?" There was a mixture of dismay and distaste in his voice.

"You had been feeling weak. Dizzy. Do you not recall?"

"Oh … yes. Concerning that … that…"

"Irishman. Moriarty."

Holmes recoiled in pain. "Say no more. But, wasn't there also here, from some years ago … that young man?"

"Young woman, Mr. Holmes," said Irene Adler, entering, dressed now in female attire.

Holmes managed to raise himself onto an elbow. "You," he said.

"Yes, I. From … not *so* many years ago. The young man who wished you goodnight." She spread her arms, displaying herself in woman's garb. "Now myself again."

"Miss Irene Adler."

"Indeed."

I indicated her appearance. "You seem to have…"

"Changed my attire?"

"Yes. In some part of the house? Are you known here?"

"No more than you and your friend."

I was taken aback. "You simply…?" I made a gesture of disrobing. I would not speak the word.

"Yes," she went on, with an innocent smile. "I simply wanted to slip into something more fitting, and I did." She seemed delighted at my discomfort. "No disrobing room is needed, Doctor. All is in the mind. The fact is, I've been roaming through the house to ascertain the whereabouts of our hosts. I'm pleased to report they are sufficiently engaged at the moment."

"'Sufficiently engaged,' Miss Adler?" I said. "For what?"

"For our purposes. Saving the life of your friend. Does the good gentleman not realize that he himself is the intended victim? You, as well?"

"We…" murmured Holmes.

"Ah, Mr. Holmes, I've been neglecting you down there. Are you able to stand on your two feet?"

"Most decidedly." Holmes rose unsteadily.

"Bravo. Because elsewhere in this house is the man who at this moment is plotting your end, and who has the power—the absolute power—to bring it about."

"There is no such thing as absolute power, Miss Adler," I said. "Except that held by our merciful Creator."

"Exactly. And yours does not intend to be merciful. Which is regrettable, for you gentlemen have much useful work yet to do. If Dr. Doyle will allow it."

"If *Dr. Doyle*…??!!"

"If he will relent, Doctor, as his wife urges. As does even his deceased father, it seems."

"I'm sure we don't know what you're talking about," I replied.

Our exploration of the subject might have gone on, but at that moment we heard the Doyles returning. Holmes and I again hurried behind the draperies. Irene Adler, to our dismay, remained where she was.

"Touie, what has gotten into you?" Doyle followed his wife into the room. "It's time for bed."

"For you as well, Arthur."

"I told you, my dear. I intend to work. To finish the Reichenbach story. Tonight."

"Then I intend to be present, my dear, to dissuade you."

"I'm thinking of your health."

"And I of the health of those two. Who unfortunately cannot look out for themselves. In any case, we leave in three days, and still so much to do. Just look at this room." She did so, which is when she spotted the violin where Holmes and I had left it. "Who left this out? I swear, Arthur, you are one of the most untidy men that ever drove a wife to distraction. Not that I am in the least conventional in that respect myself, but there is a limit, my dear."

She began moving about the room. Holmes and I poked our heads out, to watch, incredulous, as Miss Adler accompanied Madame, who seemed not to see her.

"And when," Madame continued, "I find a man who keeps his cigars in the coal-scuttle"—Miss Adler, playing auctioneer's assistant, pointed out the coal-scuttle—"his tobacco in the end of a Persian slipper"—that, too—"and his unanswered correspondence transfixed by a jackknife into the very centre of his wooden mantelpiece"—and that—"then I begin to give myself virtuous airs."

But Miss Adler needn't have bothered. Madame Doyle's mere enumeration of the items seemed sufficient for Holmes.

"But, my dear," replied Doyle, "that, all of it, is simply…"

"Me!" Holmes declared, in unison with Doyle.

"You!" said I, in chorus with both.

"Yes, you. And he," said Madame to her husband, and Miss Adler to Holmes.

"Besides, my love, you've told me all this, in exactly those words, time and time again."

"And," said Madame to her husband, and Irene Adler to me, "you have duly repeated it. In 'The Musgrave Ritual.'"

"Well, my dear, what are you to do with such an incorrigible old fool? Simply…" Dr. Doyle shook his head.

"Extraordinary," I murmured.

"Simply extraordinary, Arthur. Bedtime must wait. This room must be cleared"— Madame Doyle picked up the violin—"except for the few items I can rescue of our detective and his faithful companion." She gazed at the instrument and shook her head sadly before laying it back in its case. Doyle remained by his desk, frowning. Madame brought her eyes to his. "Coaxing yourself to work, Arthur? On that regrettable story? *Can* you?"

"I'll … it's too late for work. I'll … correspondence." He sat and took pen and paper.

Through it all, I had been signalling strenuously to Miss Adler to, for Heaven's sake, conceal herself. Instead, bestowing on me a most ingratiating smile, she went over to Doyle and proceeded to run her fingers through his hair. He brushed his head as if at a momentary fluttering. I was overcome with amazement. Holmes, for his part, merely watched. I did, however, see him study his hands again.

"I must write to Greenhough Smith at *The Strand,*" Doyle said. "Appease one's editor, as it were."

"He will be unappeasable, like the rest of us."

"Nevertheless." He took paper and started in on the letter.

"Oh, Dr. Watson," said Miss Adler, still playing with Doyle's hair, "don't look so scandalized." With that, she came over to me, and before I realized what she was about, pulled me out from the draperies and into the centre of the room, where I stood exposed, aghast, helpless. "You, also, Mr. Holmes." She started towards Holmes, but he waved her off and stepped out on his own. As I watched in complete bewilderment, and Irene Adler in complete approval, Holmes went to the desk and stood directly across from Doyle, even to the point of leaning in so he could not be missed. There was no reaction from Doyle. Miss Adler, clearly revelling in the moment, sat on the edge of Doyle's desk, swinging a leg, right at the doctor's elbow.

"Surely, Mr. Holmes," she said, "this invisibility of ours, this insubstantiality…"

"Nevertheless, Arthur," Madame Doyle said, "to Smith, as to all of us, your detective is very real, very substantial. Solid."

"… this…" said Miss Adler.

"… incorporeal state?" suggested Holmes.

"Excellent, Mr. Holmes. Our 'incorporeal state.' Surely the most striking clue of all." Miss Adler performed a pirouette before Doyle, who simply went on writing. "Whatever can it all mean?"

"It means," I said—somewhat huffily, I must admit—"it can *only* mean that you have mesmerized Dr. Doyle."

"Madame Doyle, as well? You think I have that power? No, Dr. Watson. Only this gentleman sitting here. Only he has that power."

"He is not solid, Touie," Doyle said. "I have not that power. He is simply an invention, a disembodied idea, to which I, in a regrettable state of madness, gave a body."

Meanwhile, Holmes had moved behind Dr. Doyle, intent, over his shoulder, on what he was writing.

"Gave a body to them all," Doyle continued. "The detective, his doctor friend…"

Don't forget me, silently mouthed Miss Adler.

"… that Adler woman…" Doyle shook his head ruefully and went back to his writing.

"So, Mr. Holmes, Dr. Watson," Miss Adler said, "his complete knowledge of you, his handwriting…"

"No, Touie," Doyle said. "Did not *give* them a body. *Loaned* them a body."

With a sweeping gesture, Miss Adler presented Dr. Doyle. "Behold your chronicler, Mr. Holmes."

"Excuse me, Miss Adler," I said, "*I* am Holmes's chronicler. I am the one who has shared, and written accounts of, his cases. Holmes has seen me. Writing."

"As now he sees Dr. Doyle. Writing."

"A loan, Touie, which I am now calling in. Not to be renewed."

"I tell you, Miss Adler, *I* chronicle Holmes's cases!"

"And who chronicles you, Dr. Watson?"

"I beg your pardon?"

"Dr. Watson, when did you first meet Holmes?"

"I … upon my return from the Afghan War. We took up living quarters together."

"And where was that, Doctor?"

"At 221B Baker Street."

During the foregoing, Madame Doyle had returned to the filing cabinet. She now held up a file. "*A Study in Scarlet*," she said with a tone of lament. "Where it all began, Arthur." She sighed and set it down on the table, as if reluctant to add it to the others in the box.

By now, Holmes was at the large wall map of London.

"And where, Dr. Watson, is this 221B Baker Street?" Miss Adler asked.

"In the West End of London. Everyone knows that."

"What shall we do with the London street map, dear?" Madame Doyle asked.

"Oh, leave it, I should think." Then, with a tender look at his wife, plainly full of meaning, he added, "We *shall* be back."

"*We* shall, please God. But will *they*?"

"Go to the map, Dr. Watson," Miss Adler said. "Find 221B Baker Street."

"Certainly," I replied. Holmes stepped away, leaving the map to my perusal.

"Is this the last we shall see of Baker Street, Arthur?" Madame Doyle asked her husband.

At the same moment, with my finger pressed to the spot, I turned to Miss Adler and triumphantly announced, "Baker Street."

"221B," she retorted.

Again I perused the map, but soon turned back, thoroughly confused.

"Problem, Doctor?"

"I do not … cannot… Where is…?"

"I would not waste my time, Watson," Holmes said. "As you can see, Baker Street runs…"

"… no higher," said Miss Adler, "than number 83."

"Impossible!" I declared. "Holmes and I, I assure you, took rooms—Holmes resides there to this day—upstairs in Mrs. Hudson's domicile at 221B Baker Street, in…"

"*A Study in Scarlet*," said Miss Adler.

"I was going to say," I replied with the utmost forbearance, "in the West End of London."

"Yes, Doctor, the West End of London in *A Study in Scarlet*."

As if prompted, Madame Doyle picked up the folder containing the story, and clutching it to her bosom, probed the surrounding space. Evidently discovering nothing there, she left off and gently placed the folder in the box. Immediately, she spotted another on the table. "Ah, here's *The Sign of Four*. Excellent tale."

"In which," Doyle said, a softened look in his eyes, "Watson meets his wife-to-be. His beloved Mary."

With a sigh, Madame added it to the others.

"Remember, Doctor?" Irene Adler asked me.

"How well I remember," Doyle said.

"*Remember?!*" I exclaimed. "Miss Adler, I *know*. I am, after all, married to her."

"In that case, Dr. Watson, you will know your wedding date."

"Of course. It's … it's…" I had to stop. Try as I might, I could not recall. Or … did not know? My puzzlement turned to consternation, then very quickly to alarm.

"Oh, Doctor, sorry," Miss Adler said, "that's not in *The Sign of Four*. Or elsewhere."

I turned away, unable, try as I might, to make sense of this.

"Ask *me* questions," Holmes said.

"With pleasure, Mr. Holmes." She gave him a mischievous—one might even say a wicked—look. "What is your mother's name? Your father's occupation?" Holmes stared at her blankly.

"You don't know?"

"I've never been asked." Holmes looked as if he were just discovering that fact.

"Dr. Watson never mentioned it?" She smiled. "Where are you from?"

"I … have a brother Mycroft."

"'The Greek Interpreter,'" she and Madame Doyle announced together—naming the short story—Miss Adler to Holmes, Madame Doyle to her husband as she displayed its folder.

"Ah, yes," Doyle said. "Enter brother Mycroft."

"We *all* know brother Mycroft," Miss Adler said to Holmes. "Thanks to the good doctor here."

"Which one?" Holmes said.

"Exactly, Mr. Holmes."

"Enough, Touie" Doyle said, as his wife was about to cite another file.

Miss Adler turned to me. "Mr. Holmes's mother's name. Why did you never mention it?"

"I… Why, I…"

"Because, Dr. Watson, it was never mentioned to *you*?"

"Enough, Miss Adler," said Holmes.

No," I answered. "Because it was of no concern to me! It was never pertinent to the case."

"And if it *were* pertinent? *Your* mother's name, for instance. Try."

I tried. *Tried.* And came up with nothing. All I could do was stare oafishly. At that moment, however, I was extricated from my bafflement by Madame Doyle's "What shall I do with this, Arthur?" as she took from a shelf a small wooden file-card box.

"My fact files." Doyle opened the box and riffled through the cards. "Holmes and Watson." Despite himself, a note of affection seemed to have insinuated itself into his voice. "Unused details for future reference."

"*What* future, Arthur?"

"Exactly, my dear." The note of affection had departed, replaced by one of resolve. "Throw them out." Doyle pointed to the waste basket.

"No!" I exclaimed, with the blind certainty that what the good woman held in her hands was vitally precious to Holmes and me.

"No, Arthur," Madame cried. "I cannot."

"Of what use are they to me now?" He took the file box from her.

Instinctively I reached out to stop him, but at just that moment my eye was diverted by something more immediately arresting: the sight of Holmes once again staggering weakly. I turned from the Doyles and went to my colleague, whose difficulty had brought him over to Doyle's desk and into the chair Doyle had just vacated, and from which Holmes now frantically signalled to me to go and rescue the file cards. Though myself feeling some weakness, I hastened back to Doyle.

Fortunately, Madame was already there. "No," she said. "Give it here, Arthur. I'll store them. Who knows?"

"*I* know."

"Nevertheless…" She took the file box and packed it in with the folders. "There. Rescued from oblivion." I was touched by the warmth of her tone.

I resumed my ministrations to Holmes. "Feeling better, old man? I know I do."

"But what of *this* precious object?" Madame Doyle said. The violin. She opened the case and lifted it out. "To me, this more than anything evokes Holmes's presence. I can almost hear him playing one of his favourite pieces." She raised her head as if indeed hearing it, then began to sway and hum. "Oh, yes, Arthur, real he is. As real as this instrument."

"If you insist, my dear." Doyle headed back to his chair, which to my horror was occupied by Holmes. As he was about to sit, Madame was seized by a fortuitous—albeit ill-boding—fit of coughing. Dr. Doyle rushed to her. As did I. "Oh, dear," he said. "I was afraid this might happen."

"Too much exertion," I said.

"Bedtime," he said.

Madame made a sign of protest.

"Bedtime!" we commanded.

"We can finish this tomorrow, Touie." Still she hesitated. "*Will you come?*"

"Go," I urged.

"Go," Holmes echoed.

"It's best," said Irene Adler. "Go."

"Come, my dear."

With a farewell caress, Madame laid the violin in its case and allowed her husband to lead her to the door. There she stopped and turned, and looked around the space, seeming to imbibe it. Then she followed her husband out of the room and upstairs.

Once again Holmes examined his hands, as though they were some foreign object. I, for my part, had no time to probe the events of the last few minutes. My interest was only to retrieve the file box from its cardboard tomb, which I did with great dispatch. I extracted a handful of index cards, which I began going though avidly. Soon I had the one I was looking for.

"Mary and I were married on October eleventh!"

"An autumn wedding," Miss Adler said. "How lovely."

"Indeed it was." I paused to think. "Was it?"

Irene Adler began going through the cards. "Your mother's name, Mr. Holmes, is Margaret. Margaret Joan."

"Ah," Holmes said. "Very euphonious," He was now poking at his arms, his torso, his face.

"You were born in Yorkshire. Raised in East Sussex. No doubt you moved there as a child. You and brother Mycroft."

"No doubt."

By now I had perused several more cards. "How does that man know all this? And so completely controls our lives? So completely defines them?"

"Who is it knows our lives, Dr. Watson?" Miss Adler asked. "And defines them? And then controls them?"

"Only our Creator in Heaven, Madame."

"Oh?" she answered. "What of our creator…"

"… on Earth."

"Exactly, Mr. Holmes."

"My head is clear. The evidence points." Holmes rose and looked slowly around the room, taking in each object. "So it is," he muttered. "As if newly born."

Had I heard right?

"But it is beyond belief," he continued, as if denying what he was admitting. "One of his 'people.' A *character.*"

"In the world Dr. Doyle has created for us," Miss Adler offered quietly.

"Created us for," Holmes replied querulously.

"Ah, Mr. Holmes, you do understand."

"I do, Miss Adler. Accepting, however, is quite another matter." He sank back into the desk chair. "How could I have been so dense? I kept coming up to it, but my mind would not—"

"Do not berate yourself, Mr. Holmes. How could one possibly deduce, whatever the evidence, that one is not … actual?"

"Are you saying," I asked, my indignation rising, "that I … we … are mere figments of—?"

"Not at all," said Miss Adler. "I do not consider myself a figment, and certainly not mere. A grand creation, rather."

"Of Dr. Doyle's mind," Holmes said.

"Yes. He thinks, therefore I am." She shrugged. "What of it?"

"*What of it*?!" I exclaimed. "You say that we"—I hunted for the word—"*inhabit* … a world that is not the … the …?" This time I had the word, but could not bring myself to utter it.

"But, Dr. Watson, for us it *is* the real world."

"For Dr. Doyle, however," Holmes said, looking despondent, "and for others"—he made a sweeping gesture, indicating the room and what I took to be the world beyond it—"a fictional creation."

"These," I said ruefully, "are the fruits of your synthetic method."

"And the analytic."

"I absolutely refuse! I live in the real world. The *only* real world!"

"Yes, Dr. Watson, the only real world of *The Sign of Four,* plus the twelve stories of *The Adventures of Sherlock Holmes* and the eleven stories of *The Memoirs*—"

"*The Memoirs* contains only ten stories."

"The eleventh is in progress, Doctor … the crucial one." She pointed to the green folder. "The one Dr. Doyle plans to finish without delay."

"Let him then, the plagiarist."

"You do not seem to grasp, dear sir, that if anyone is the plagiarist, it is you."

"And if anyone is the helpless fool," said Holmes, "it is I."

"You must not think that, Mr. Holmes."

"Very well for you to say, Miss Adler. This fact of our 'existence' is something you have always known."

"Indeed, I was not given time to know any other. One story."

"We, however, *were* given time," Holmes replied. "So many … *stories*." My friend's pain in uttering this last word was palpable. "Deluded, we were. For us, a most horrifying revelation."

"But it need not be."

"How can it be otherwise, Madame?" I asked, interrupting myself in the course of prodding my own arms, face, and torso.

"Are you not a practicing Christian, Doctor, content to live under the will of God?"

"Most certainly."

"So, be content to live, instead, under the will of Doyle. Which you've been doing anyway all your literary life. One reality for another. It's of no matter. For, who knows, even Dr. Doyle, Madame Doyle, the 'others' out there"—she copied Holmes's world-encompassing gesture—"may themselves be the unsuspecting creation of a reality beyond the one *they* know."

"Interesting notion, that," said Holmes.

"*Comforting* notion, that," Miss Adler replied. "Exhilarating even. For, who else ever gets to meet his maker?"

"All Christians, Madame."

"While alive, Doctor?" She saw her point sink home. "But, gentlemen, does it matter, really? You, Doctor. Have you ever felt yourself constricted or limited in any way? Or you, Mr. Holmes?"

"No," replied Holmes, who, having reassumed his customary nature, had embarked on a meticulous tour of the room, clearly with a new purpose in mind. "Quite the contrary, I must admit."

"Indeed, given that your creator has fashioned you into one of the most brilliant men in England. Would you rather take your chance in Dr. Doyle's world? The fact is, you live a life most men can only envy."

"For not much longer, however"

"And whither thou goest, Holmes, there go I."

"Not exactly, Watson. I go to the bottom of Reichenbach Falls."

"And I to eternity at the bottom of that box."

"With your beloved Mary," Irene Adler said. "If that's any consolation."

"In either case, Miss Adler," Holmes said, "neither of us will be heard from again."

"Oh, again, certainly. Not *anew*. A kind of artistic purgatory, the place in Dr. Doyle's firmament where I have existed ever since you, Doctor Watson ... *he*, that is ... completed the story in which I flourished. A home, not unpleasant, for retired characters, and for those in the wings. All of whom have been helplessly observing his recent plans for you, and elected me to bring you here—which I have duly accomplished—where we three can still share space, I in retirement, you still on the street, as it were—because we need you to stop our creator from casting away his creation: our world ... our reality. Even though, as I say, we retired ones shall likely never appear anew to your readers."

"Doyle's readers," I said.

"On his plane only, Doctor. On this, *your* readers. Yes, he moved your hand. But *your* hand moved."

"Well, have no fear, it shall never move to send Holmes to the bottom of that cataract."

"I appreciate the sentiment, Watson, but I expect Dr. Doyle's hand will prove the stronger. Resistance would seem to be out of the question."

"Am I hearing surrender, Holmes? Surely you have something in mind."

"No, Watson, I have nothing in mind. Nothing."

"Are we helpless, then?"

"I'm wrestling with the possibility."

"That we are helpless, Mr. Holmes? *Are* we? Are *you*?"

"Are we not, Miss Adler? Am *I* not? Why struggle, when all is unreal?"

"Why struggle, indeed, Mr. Holmes," came a low mocking voice from the doorway, followed by a laugh devoid of humour. I froze, thinking it was Dr. Doyle, surprised that he would have left his bed and returned to the room from which he and his wife had so recently, so agitatedly, departed. But when I turned to face him, when we all turned, we saw not Dr. Doyle, but a dim figure, a man extremely tall and thin, with a forehead that domed out in a white curve, and eyes deeply sunken in his head. From what we could see, he was clean-shaven, pale, ascetic-looking. His shoulders and back were rounded, and he had puckered eyes, which kept peering and blinking at us. He wore a dark suit of good cut and an unbuttoned black frock coat which came nearly to his ankles.

I was struck dumb by this sudden apparition out of nowhere, and by the look of him. Miss Adler, I noticed, seemed less astonished, and less impressed. There was a stern expression on her face, which led me to believe that she knew this person, if person he was, and that she was not amused to see him here. It was Holmes's reaction, however, that most caught my attention. At the first sight of the figure, Holmes had recoiled and stiffened in place, as one might do before a viper that has suddenly risen in one's path—which might well have been so, for the man's face protruded forward somewhat and constantly oscillated from side to side in a curiously reptilian fashion. In any case, it was clear to me that Holmes regarded this figure as an adversary, and a dangerous one at that.

Several seconds elapsed with no word spoken. At length, Miss Adler came forward. "What are you doing here?" she demanded. "You were to remain with the others. Especially you."

"The 'others?'" The figure made a contemptuous flick of the hand. "You mean those who have no future?"

"I mean those who have done great service," Miss Adler replied. "Those who have gone before. Those who have lived."

"As do these two standing before me. As shall I."

"As *shall* you? Live?" said Holmes, who by now had regained his composure. He smiled ever so slightly, and ever so slightly nodded. "I assume then, that I am addressing one Professor Moriarty."

I marvelled that Holmes had no difficulty this time in speaking the dreaded name. On the contrary, he seemed to be standing tall—taller than I'd seen him all that trying day—as though now that he had determined whom he was facing, he relished where he was and what might ensue. The gentleman made no reply, nor did Holmes venture to say anything more. The two simply stood where they were, taking the measure of each other.

"Yes," said Miss Adler. "It is he."

The professor offered a curt nod.

"Why have you come here?" Miss Adler asked again. Professor Moriarty ignored her question, offering instead a show of defiance. But it was Miss Adler's own defiance that now presented itself. "Go back to them, you wretch, back to the realm of the unformed and the half-formed whence you came. For you know you are no more than that, if even that."

The professor bristled at her harshness. "'Whence … I … came,'" he said, with the same mocking dismissiveness as before. "That is for them, not me. Do you really think me bound by the rules that bind others?"

"No 'rules.' That is the realm to which you are consigned."

"At present only, dear lady. Soon to be liberated into full existence. As you and your associates here well know."

"Know?" Holmes said. "*What* do we know?"

"What Dr. Doyle intends."

"Dr. Doyle?" Holmes said. "You know Dr. Doyle? *How* do you know Dr. Doyle?"

I could not quite follow the line of Holmes's questioning, but concluded that he was attempting to draw the professor out, hoping he would let slip some useful bit of information or would falter in some other advantageous way. I had seen Holmes do this before, when he found himself in intellectual combat with an adversary and was probing for whatever opening might present itself.

Professor Moriarty, however, was not so easily taken in. "In the same way you do, Mr. Holmes. And your faithful colleague here. And for that matter, you, dear Miss Adler."

If the professor's familiarity towards her was intended to distress the good lady, it failed. She wagged a corrective finger at the intruder. "Not so, Professor. Indeed, not at all. Look at us. Creatures of the imagination, to be sure, but whole, fully realized, warm-blooded. We live—my two associates here—or have lived—myself—and continue today. You can make no such claim. Look at yourself."

Professor Moriarty did nothing.

"I mean that literally," she said. "Look."

Though clearly not wanting to accede to any command from this woman, the professor glanced down at his hands, the only visible part of his body other than his face—though in regard to the latter, I doubt a mirror would have availed.

"Pale," Miss Adler said. "Because bloodless. Bloodless…"

Hearing her words, I perceived now the wraithlike quality of the man, an air about him of translucency. Miss Adler's words appeared to have had a singular effect on him as well. He stiffened a moment, then lifted his head, an unwavering look of pugnacity on his face.

"… until and unless," Miss Adler continued, "Dr. Doyle sees fit to infuse you with the fluid of creation."

"Creation that only he can grant," Holmes said.

"And which only I can chronicle," I added.

"So, you see," Miss Adler said, "you have no standing here."

"Not so," Moriarty said, his threatening tone unmistakable. "I will have life, and I am here to claim it."

"You will have," Miss Adler replied, "whatever life, in quality or duration, Dr. Doyle chooses to give you. At the moment, however, you are no more than a notion. A mere figment." She managed a glance at Holmes, who, despite the tenseness of the moment, was clearly amused by the good lady's comment. As was I. For the as-yet-unrealized Professor Moriarty was indeed a mere figment, and Miss Adler—Holmes and myself, as well—was determined that he remain so. I felt certain, however, that this gentleman would not easily accept that state of affairs. Already I could see him evaluating the situation, much as I often watched Holmes himself, in the midst of a predicament, deliberate a course of action.

"Your words do not deter me, Miss Adler," our visitor said. "Nor yours, Mr. Holmes … Dr. Watson. For me, it is only a matter of time. I know as well as you what Dr. Doyle is bent on accomplishing. This very evening."

"There you are wrong," I said. "I regret to inform you that the good gentleman has retired for the night."

"Regret not, Doctor," Moriarty replied. "With us, time is relative, is it not? He will."

"Not if I can help it," Holmes said.

"And what can you do about it, Mr. Holmes? As I've learned from my time 'in the wings,' as Miss Adler puts it, my 'notional' time"—this with a disdainful glare at her—"it is Dr. Doyle, not you, who decides what is to play out."

"In your case, evil," I said.

"Ah, yes. 'Evil.' Call it what you will, Doctor, but I put it to you that evil, too, must be given its due. Must be allowed to live. For it lives in the world of Dr. Doyle, does it not? The so-called real world? Thrives, in fact."

"Which is why it is our duty to stamp it out where we can."

"Courageous words, Doctor, but even you do not have the power to do that. Unless…" He stopped, letting the moment hang.

"Unless what?" I said, and at once felt I had played into the professor's hands. Clever man.

He nodded, as if to thank me. "Unless that other doctor, he who has retired for the night, he who has fashioned you, who has fashioned us all—including me even in my 'incomplete' state—wills it."

Again, I could not stop myself. "Wills what?"

"Wills the combat to come. And I say he does will it, and shall, whatever he intends ultimately. You three are bent on preventing that, but I intend to thwart you. I have said that I will have life, as fully as Miss Adler has had and you now have, and you, Mr. Holmes, are as helpless to stop me as you are to stop Dr. Doyle." Moriarty smiled in triumph.

"You are getting ahead of yourself," replied Holmes. For the last minutes, he had been silently contemplating the professor's utterances, as well as the man himself, and I sensed from his bearing that he had found, courtesy of the professor, the opening he had been seeking. "If I am helpless," he said, "if Dr. Doyle does indeed give you life … a brief life it will be. One that will end almost as soon as it begins."

"You don't know that," Moriarty said.

"Oh, I do know it," Holmes replied. "You may take my word for it."

I glanced to the desk where the green folder lay. Was it possible that Moriarty knew its contents, and that even in his half-realized state he might have influence over it?

"For unless I am able to deter Dr. Doyle," Holmes went on, "a speedy and violent death awaits you."

"Does it, now?" the professor said, seemingly amused. "If so, Mr. Holmes, be assured that I will take you with me."

"And be assured, Professor, that I would gladly accompany you, if by doing so I rid England and the world of so iniquitous a creature as yourself."

Moriarty appeared to take Holmes's words as a compliment. Holmes seized the opportunity. "And a pity that would be, my dear Professor, after only a brief appearance in but one story. So brilliant a person as yourself, so adept a manipulator of people and events, surely deserves more of a career than that."

It was clear from the professor's silence that he agreed—that Holmes's lure might be having its effect. Indeed, how often had I heard Holmes observe that a singularly unfailing way to disarm even the most brilliant of criminals was through their innate vanity about their very brilliance.

"Whereas," Holmes continued, "if you wisely desist from your attempt to impede my efforts as regards Dr. Doyle, I offer the possibility, the *possibility*, I say, that in preventing the good doctor from fulfilling his plan regarding me, I may thereby prevent him from fulfilling his plan regarding you"—here Moriarty attempted to interrupt, but Holmes persisted—"*meaning* ... there may be many more adventures to be recounted by my worthy colleague here"—Holmes graciously nodded to me—"in which you will have the opportunity to thrive, in perpetual combat with us."

Moriarty weighed Holmes's words and appeared about to accede to his advice, but something—pride, stubbornness, or perhaps simply a dogged refusal to give in to anyone's wishes but his own—pulled him back from that unspeakable brink. "Nicely said, Mr. Holmes, but all to no avail. You are correct in the course of action Dr. Doyle must take, but as I have said, I do not require your help. I am more than capable of accomplishing alone what is necessary with regard to Dr. Doyle's, or, as you say, Dr. Watson's, future compositional endeavours."

Holmes and I were put off by this refusal, but Miss Adler again leapt into the breach. She burst out laughing—a laugh which began as sheer enjoyment but quickly transformed itself into biting ridicule. A most unladylike tone, I could not help thinking, but welcome for all that.

"'Capable,' Professor?" she said. "You may potentially be the mastermind of European crime, brilliant in thought, planning, and execution, but I perceive a lack: you do not listen well. Did you not hear, or comprehend, what I told you earlier? Or did you simply ignore it, confusing the mere promise of power with the actual possession of it, like one inebriated on the mere aroma of alcoholic spirits? Whatever, let me state plainly again: You, as you stand there, can do nothing vis-à-vis Dr. Doyle. You doubtless have some plan in mind, some strategy for achieving your wish as regards the good doctor, but that matters not. And the simple reason is that you do not ... yet ... exist. In any world. You are a non entity, with no more power than a light breeze. Is that understood, or need I put it otherwise?"

For the first time since he had arrived among us, Professor Moriarty's composure seemed to take flight, long enough, at least, for him to appear apprehensive, anxious ... perhaps fearful.

"Are you too unwitting, my dear Professor," continued Miss Adler, "to realize that at this moment your greatest allies are standing before you?"

"Indeed that is so," Holmes said. "Have I not shown you that we have a common goal? You wish to live. I wish to go on living. You, however, must accept that you can do nothing to effect that end, as Miss Adler has so accurately stated. I, on the other hand, can do much. Need I repeat that it is in your best interest, therefore, to cease this attempt to obstruct me in pursuit of my own? For if and as I, as well as Dr. Watson, enjoy life, so too might you. Only if Dr. Doyle continues in his compositional endeavours, as you so succinctly put it, do you stand the possibility of breathing the same air as we. No promise. I can act for myself only, you understand. But it is your sole hope."

"And how, precisely, do you propose to achieve your purpose?" Moriarty asked, holding on to his obduracy like a dog to the trouser leg of a burglar.

Holmes said nothing. Suddenly I realized with some alarm that he did not know.

"You do not know, do you?" Moriarty said, shaking his head in mock pity. "As you were saying when I arrived, you are helpless. You have no means, and no plan, for gaining access to Dr. Doyle. You are where you are, at his beck and call, and he is where he is: unreachable. A circuit, as it were, but flawed. Open."

"Well put, Professor. But do you really think that I, in a matter of life and death such as this, will not find the way to close that circuit? You have no choice but to accept that I can and will, and to do as I suggest—if, that is, you hope to pursue your criminal proclivities in future creations of Dr. Doyle…"

"Through me," I said.

"… in combat with myself," Holmes continued. "Does not the prospect please you? I know it does me."

The inescapability and temptation of Holmes's words seemed too much for the professor. Though he maintained his antagonistic expression, there was—in a slight but unmistakable droop of his body—acceptance. I saw him waver.

As did Miss Adler. "You are an intelligent man, Professor, are you not?" she said, clearly adopting Holmes's tactic of flattery. "More than intelligent. Able to observe, to perceive, to weigh … to decide. You observe the circumstance here. You perceive the relative position of yourself versus us. You weigh on one side of the scale the factors against you. On the other, the benefits of deciding wisely. Which I know you will do."

Still the gentleman hesitated.

"Or," said the indefatigable lady, "you will remain here and risk going down in literary history, if at all, as no more than an annoyance, a pest, a stillborn idea. Better to depart now, and thus take your chance at everlasting literary renown."

"Dependent on Mr. Holmes here," observed the professor morosely.

"That may very well be," Holmes replied, "but as I said, in doing my utmost for myself and Dr. Watson, I will be doing my utmost for you."

"For which, Mr. Holmes, I will do my utmost to repay you."

It was not said kindly.

"I am sure you will," Holmes replied. "I look forward to it."

"Indeed, do. I would have it no other way." The professor nodded solemnly. "I leave the field to you. For the present." And with those words, Professor Moriarty retreated a step, turned from us, and already beginning to evanesce as he reached the doorway, passed out of sight.

III

For a full quarter-minute, we three stood motionless, voice-less, then as one let out a great sigh of relief. Only as we drew breath again did we realize how very tense we had been through the entire encounter.

"A most entertaining interlude," Holmes said at last.

More than that, I thought. We had met our adversary, had contended with him, and had come through. "Where does he go now?" I asked Miss Adler.

"Oh, most likely to scowl and scheme in some dark corner of the world in which budding creations wait to be born. In his case, to the nether area where evil abides until it can spring itself on the world."

"In any event," I said, "I commend you, Miss Adler, and you, Holmes my dear friend, on so brilliantly dealing with the man. I must say, when he appeared I was filled with dread that our efforts to this point would go for naught."

"Which they yet may do," Holmes said, "inasmuch as we still do not have a strategy for altering Dr. Doyle's course of action. And even if we somehow manage to arrive at one, and Dr. Doyle contin-ues concocting adventures in which we function, they will now very possibly include Professor Moriarty."

"A *fully realized* Professor Moriarty," Miss Adler added, "which will make him a most dangerous adversary. Not as summarily dealt with as on this occasion."

"But surely, Holmes, no match for you."

"I look forward, Watson, to discovering if that is so. But should we be fortunate enough eventually to defeat him, who knows how much havoc he will have wreaked by then? Whatever, my friends, at the moment it behooves us to escape the fate Dr. Doyle intends for us, and we must find the means to do so this very evening"—he tapped the green folder—"in the story contained in this manuscript. Featuring the fully realized professor's first appearance."

"And his last?" said Miss Adler, repeating Holmes's gesture of a fall into the chasm.

Holmes shrugged. "We have no definite sway over that, as I explained to the gestating professor."

"But"—I copied the over-the-edge gesture—"surely not you, Holmes."

"That is a given, Watson. But … how to do it?"

"Which is exactly where we were," said Miss Adler, "when the professor paid his visit."

"Quite so. As I recall, you had at that moment asked if we are helpless. And I had just said—indeed I say now—that yes, helpless we very well may be, inasmuch as Dr. Doyle, at present more our adversary than the professor, dwells in a world significantly more real than ours, and thereby impenetrable. We were able to overcome the obstacle of Professor M because he exists in our world … or will. Regrettably, he is one of us. The obstacle of Dr. Doyle, however, is of a different order, and it is against that far more solid impediment that I feel the uncertainty, the unreality, of our footing."

"Not entirely so, Mr. Holmes," said Miss Adler. "May I remind you of someone in that significantly more real world to whom all of this"—she indicated the box of story folders and the file cabinet beyond it—"is only too real? Someone for whom the fate of Dr. Doyle's creation is also a matter of life and death?"

As if summoned, Madame Doyle appeared in the doorway, and Miss Adler, like a courtroom barrister presenting a clinching piece of evidence, presented her to us. We watched as Madame, who appeared to have recovered from her coughing spell, took a moment to gather both herself and a sense of the room, then with a furtive glance back, went to the violin case and lifted out the violin. She put her forehead to the instrument for several seconds, as if to commune with its very being, then cradled it lovingly before uttering a long sigh and laying it back in its case.

"She loves that violin," I whispered to Holmes.

Madame now moved to the locked bookcase and peered through its glass door, before laying her hand on it and giving way to another deep sigh.

"Curious," Holmes murmured.

She came away from the bookcase. Her eyes roamed the study, as if she were imprinting on her memory a place she would be seeing no more. Then, as suddenly as she'd appeared, she left the room and returned upstairs.

"Of course!" Holmes said. "This bookcase. The only place in the room Dr. Doyle assiduously keeps locked. Where he guards his poems more than his other writing. Why?"

"I'd say that lies in the nature of poets and poetry," Miss Adler said. "Those poems likely contain Dr. Doyle's innermost thoughts."

"I venture to say you're right, Madame. Though literature has never been one of my strong points."

"You're joking, Mr. Holmes. Literature is your very being."

Holmes conceded the point with an amused nod. Even I appreciated the good lady's poke at my colleague.

"It would seem obvious," Miss Adler said, "that Madame Doyle…"

"Bless her," I said.

"… has sensed the great importance of those poems."

"Indeed, she has," I said. "Shortly before you arrived, her husband was pointing out their importance."

"Judging from her actions," Holmes said, "I would say she has sensed more than that." He indicated the three of us. "The need—hers and ours—is mutual, is it not? Oh, the dear lady."

"Well, then, Mr. Holmes, which is it to be? *Are* you helpless?"

"Helpless? Am I Holmes? Have you ever known me, in the face of a crime, real or contemplated, to despair of the solution?"

"Never!" I exclaimed.

"Bravo, Mr. Holmes. We expected no less of you."

"Our way is clear. Madame Doyle has shown us. As has the professor." Holmes went to the bookcase and scanned it, top to bottom. "How to foil the Reichenbach scheme," he mused, "and thereby keep Dr. Doyle engaged in further Holmesian exploits."

"Not quite, Mr. Holmes," said Miss Adler. "We must certainly prevent the crime at Reichenbach. But we must be mindful as well that Mrs. Doyle is a very sick woman…"

"Indeed, she is," I said.

"… whose cure depends on Dr. Doyle's giving her his full attention. In Switzerland. We are obliged to help her. Therefore, until she is cured—or the unthinkable occurs—Dr. Doyle must be granted a hiatus from his creative endeavours."

"You demonstrate an admirable sensitivity, Miss Adler," Holmes said. "And you are right, of course."

"Of course. So, we must devise a way to save all of you. Kill two birds with one stone, as it were. Or three, in this case."

"Miss Adler, I beg you."

"Oh. Of course, Doctor. Sorry."

"We shall indeed proceed delicately," Holmes said. "And, Miss Adler, we shall want your further help in this. You'll remain with us a while longer?"

"Remain? Mr. Holmes, I would not miss this for the world. Either one."

"Excellent." Holmes produced his penknife, and was about to address himself to the bookcase lock when he stopped and turned to Miss Adler. "You don't mind breaking the law? Having on occasion done so in aid of others, I see no reason to refrain when I and my esteemed colleague are the ones in peril."

"Not in the least, Mr Holmes."

"Nor running a chance of arrest?"

"Not in a good cause," I said.

"Oh, the cause is excellent."

"Then I'm your man."

"And I."

"Excellent, Miss Adler."

"But, gentlemen," the good lady said, "you forget yourselves. *What* law? *What* chance of arrest?" She looked at each of us in turn. "So, you see the advantage?"

I must confess I was beginning to.

"All right then, my friends," Holmes said. "To work."

Holmes found the bookcase lock as easy to solve as that of the desk drawer. He opened the glass door—"Here they are"—and brought the portfolio of poems to Doyle's desk. He sat. Miss Adler and I took positions on either side, peering over his shoulder.

"And here it is. 'The Inner Room.' What Dr. Doyle read to Madame Doyle.

> *'It is mine—the little chamber,*
> *Mine alone.*
> *I had it from my forbears*
> *Years agone.'"*

"'It is mine—the little chamber,'" Holmes murmured, pondering. "What little chamber?"

"A secret room, perhaps?" I suggested.

Miss Adler leaned in to read.

> "'*Yet within its walls I see*
> *A most motley company…*'"

She pondered a moment. "Sounds rather public."

"… 'a most…motley…company,'" the three of us muttered over and over. "Could that be us?" I asked.

"And others," Miss Adler said. "His 'characters.'"

I frowned. "Motley company, indeed."

Miss Adler returned to the first line.

> "'*It is mine—the little chamber,*
> *Mine alone.*'"

Her eyes roamed the study. "He means this room."

"Consider again, Miss Adler." Holmes pointed to the next lines. "'*I had it from my forbears years agone.*' Not this chamber"—Holmes indicated the study—"but … *this.*" He touched his head. "As you yourself said, the inner working of the poet's mind. Most instructive, therefore, is the line which follows his reference to the motley crew."

"'*And they one and all claim me as their own.*'" Miss Adler stared at the words, then looked up, her face suddenly aglow with understanding. "He is saying that the creator is not independent of his creations."

"Or at least," Holmes concluded, "*feels* he is not. Come, let us see what else we have here." He distributed some of the other poems. "But quickly, my friends, for as we frolic poetically, lives hang in the balance, beginning with mine." He delved into his batch, and Miss

Adler and I into our own. A minute or two, and then: "Aha! Might this be it?"

We looked at the poem Holmes had put on the desk, and read in unison:

> "'*So read I this, and as I try*
> *To write it clear again,*
> *I feel a second finger lie*
> *Above mine on the pen.*'"

"'So read I this,'" I repeated, "'and as I try to write it clear again…'"

"It's like the one we just read," Miss Adler said. "Dr. Doyle himself, writing about writing."

"In this case, about re-writing."

"The bane of our existence," I said.

"The salvation of ours," said Holmes, brandishing the poem.

"Indeed?"

"Indeed, Miss Adler. 'I feel a second finger lie above mine on the pen.' Whose second finger?"

"Ours. Of course!"

"The motley company," I ventured.

Holmes returned to the first poem. "'*And they one and all claim me as their own.*' By one and all, you see, laying a second finger…"

"A writing finger," said Miss Adler, her excitement growing.

"… on his," concluded Holmes. "We have it!"

"We do?" I asked.

"Recall my method, Watson. How often have I said, 'When you have eliminated the impossible, whatever remains, however improbable, must be the truth?'"

"Often."

"But what impossible have you eliminated, Mr. Holmes?"

"To begin with, Miss Adler, any hope of physical escape. Dr. Doyle holds us in captivity, prisoners of his imagination, a captivity as unbreakable as if we were chained in the deepest dungeon. Next, any hope to resist him. He controls our actions just as he controls our place. Third, any hope to rewrite on our own what is to be my last adventure—this 'Final Problem.' As we have learned, he, not my esteemed colleague—my deepest sympathy, Watson—is final arbiter of what goes onto the page."

"What 'improbable' remains then?"

"Hopefully, Miss Adler, enough for us to fashion the necessary rescue. We start with the poems. Like us, the product of his imagination. An imagination teeming with fears, hopes, events, and characters of all sorts, formed and half-formed."

"Sounds a very crowded neighbourhood," I said.

"Just so, Watson. A neighbourhood. The neighbourhood of the mind."

"Doyle's mind."

"But *our* neighbourhood."

"Where Baker Street runs to 221B," said Miss Adler.

"Indeed," I replied, that discovery still smarting.

"And where," Holmes said, "its creator walks in fear."

"He does?" said Miss Adler and I both.

"Yes. Fear that his creatures will 'one and all claim him as their own.' That the act of creation will not be his alone."

"That he will," Miss Adler said, working it out as she went along, "feel the second finger…"

"… ours …"

"… pressing …"

"… above his on the pen."

"But, Holmes," I said, "you've just pointed out that we are powerless to rewrite this final story of his. And as for our finger on his, have we not determined, to my dismay, that it is *his* hand pushes *mine*?"

"And thus, Watson, you have eliminated the last of the impossibles. We cannot force him to write. Yet he feels our hand on his. So, what remains? What meaning, however improbable?"

Irene Adler paced. "That Dr. Doyle, even as he chooses what his literary creations think and do…"

"… finds his choices are being chosen *by them*!" I blinked, taken aback at my sudden intuition.

"And that, my friends," said Holmes, "is our reality. So, it is for us to help him choose my fate. Or in this instance, re-choose."

"I think you've hit it, old man."

"But," Holmes mused, "how to manage it? I must confess, operating from one realm into another is not something with which I'm especially conversant. As the professor so aptly put it: 'an open circuit.' Running, at present, in one direction only. Like a half-circle which must be completed. By me. But how do I cross that boundary? *Can* I cross it?" He looked off, as if the answer might lie on the air, but shook his head. "A three-pipe problem, if ever there was one." His hand went to his pocket, from which he took out his old black pipe, which he perused now as if it were a talisman of thought— which in a sense it was, being the pipe he usually called on when meditating a course of action. He patted his other pockets. "Hmm, I seem to have left my tobacco behind."

"At 221B?" Miss Adler said. "Well, is not this…?" Her gesture swept the room. From the mantel, she took the cloth Persian slipper containing Doyle's tobacco pouch and offered it to Holmes.

"So it seems."

"And the tobacco, Mr. Holmes? Similar to your blend?"

He sniffed the tobacco. "It *is* my blend. I trust Dr. Doyle will not begrudge me a pipeful." He started to fill his pipe, then suddenly stopped. He sniffed the tobacco again. "But of course. What other *could* it be?" He contemplated the tobacco a few moments, then took in the room, revisiting in turn the various items in it. "Yes. Yes.

Yes! The objects. The furnishings. One and the same. Ours as much as his. We are not only here; we are at 221B. And when at 221B, we are also here. And so, we hold these things, touch them, move them about. For they are ours, even as they are his." A look of awe filled his face, an expression I had seldom seen him wear. "But the question remains," he went on, "how do I…?" His words trailed off into silent musing. He brought his hand to his brow and lowered his head, as if looking inward, his concentration intense.

During the foregoing, Irene Adler had slipped over to Dr. Doyle's desk, where she now stood swaying ever so slightly, as in a trance.

"Miss Adler?" I said.

She seemed not to hear. Nor to see, for her eyes were closed. "Concentrating. Sensing. Probing outer reaches."

"I prefer deductive thought," Holmes muttered.

"Invisible forces," she intoned.

"Visible evidence."

"Sshh! I sense something. A powerful object. Pulling me. Pulling us all. Come closer." I did as she bade. Despite himself, Holmes followed suit. "Do you not feel it?" Miss Adler whispered.

Solemnly, I nodded. "Holmes?"

"I … must confess, I do."

"Of course you do," said Miss Adler.

"And, I must confess, I felt the same sensation earlier," Holmes said, "when we travelled to this place and arrived in this room." He appeared discomfited by the fact.

"As did I, Holmes. But where does it come from?"

Rather than answer, Miss Adler turned a steady gaze on my colleague, seeming to will him into action. As if drawn, Holmes moved to the small figurine on the shelf. He studied it, then lifted it, reached in, and as Miss Adler nodded approvingly, extracted the necklace we had seen Madame Eneri place there. Holmes held it up. Dangling from it was an oval-shaped pendant of a translucent amber colour.

"Behold, gentlemen," Miss Adler said, a triumphant expression on her face.

I was astonished. She seemed to have known it would draw us there. But I had little time to reflect on that, because almost at once I found myself caught, in fact near-hypnotized, by the pendant's slow oscillation back and forth. "It appears to be a charm of some sort."

"An amulet, Doctor." Miss Adler gently took the chain from Holmes's hands. Immediately its spell subsided. "A talisman."

"Why ... yes," I said. "I heard of such in Afghanistan. An object supposedly possessing magical powers. What do you make of it, Holmes?"

"You know my opinion of 'matters spiritualistic.'"

"Mr. Holmes," said Miss Adler, "as Dr. Doyle's creation, are not *you* matter spiritualistic?" Holmes grunted a reluctant assent.

Miss Adler held the ornament out to the two of us, letting it dangle tantalizingly. "Mr. Holmes, Dr. Watson: know that I and the rest of Dr. Doyle's characters invested this object with our fears and our most fervent hopes. Only then was I dispatched with it to summon you."

"Ah!" I exclaimed. "Eneri ... Irene! Irene ... Eneri! I *knew* I had seen that lady before."

"Indeed, yes," said Holmes.

"How very clever, Miss Adler." The good lady accepted my compliment with a pleased smile. More than a compliment, in truth: my respect and admiration, which—it must have been obvious—were growing every minute. "But how...?"

"How did it come about?"

I nodded.

"Quite straightforward. Dr. Doyle was extremely eager to see his deceased father. He still is, in fact ... and was therefore extremely desperate to engage a medium who could accomplish that other-worldly phenomenon. Being an other-worldly phenomenon myself, if I may so put it—and one on whom he had, moreover, bestowed a talent for disguise— I had little difficulty transmuting into the spirit and guise of one Madame Eneri, séance medium, and this afternoon presenting myself at his doorstep."

"Did he not wonder at that?" I asked.

"On the contrary. Dr. Doyle was so primed to see what he wished to see—I daresay you gentlemen have noted his heightened mental state—that the merest hint of an exotic presence was enough to effect my manifestation before him. He was, as it were, easily accessible to this denizen of the realm of the imagination. I expected no less. Have I not already pointed out that he and his fellow beings are perhaps themselves the denizens of some other realm's imagination? Our reality within his reality within some other reality, within yet another … et cetera. With commerce between realities quite achievable."

"Like the image in mirrors facing each other," I said.

"Or," Holmes offered, "one of those fanciful paintings that shows the same painting showing *that* same painting, showing … and so on."

"Perhaps endlessly," said Miss Adler. "In such a universe, what are the rules?" We waited to hear. Miss Adler shook her head. "All things are possible, are they not?"

"A useful observation, that," said Holmes.

"Dr. Doyle was so delighted by my arrival," Miss Adler went on, "that he immediately rearranged this room—fortunately Madame Doyle, so kindred a spirit to her husband, acceded to his wild fancy—and we began. But instead of serving the doctor by summoning Charles Doyle, I served those who had sent me here by summoning you and Mr. Holmes."

"But of course." Holmes said. He went to the round table and peered at the tablecloth. "One man … and one woman. Madame Eneri left no impression."

"My oversight. It's of no matter. What does matter is that I and my fellow characters are invested in this object dangling from my fingers, and through it in you. That is why it brought you here today. And has kept you here."

"And," said Holmes, "will be the means to get us safely out."

"It *is* powerfully suggestive." Miss Adler handed the pendant back to Holmes, who took it gingerly, clearly now in awe of both its power and its constituency.

"Let us review," Holmes said. "Watson, what was Dr. Doyle doing when we arrived?"

"He was seated at this table. Engaged in a séance."

"And," Holmes said, "this object was present?"

"More than present, Mr. Holmes," said Miss Adler. "It was central to the event."

"Quite so." Holmes placed the ornament on the round table. "Suppose, Madame, you are Dr. Doyle. You enter this room. This object lies here. Can you, Dr. Doyle, see it?"

"Of course I can."

"At the same time, you, Irene Adler, are standing where you are now. Can you, Dr. Doyle, see Irene Adler?"

"Only if I, Dr. Doyle, am in a highly suggestible state of mind— as when Madame Eneri first appeared—and Miss Adler is actively in my mind at that moment. As when, Mr. Holmes, he waved that manuscript at you and quoted my 'Good night, Mr. Holmes.' Re-entered my world, as it were."

"Crossed the barrier."

"In *this* direction."

"But at the very moment he enters this room—is Miss Adler in his mind?"

"Actively? At that moment? No reason to think so."

"So, if you, Irene Adler, were not on Dr. Doyle's mind at the moment he entered the room…"

"… I would be invisible to him."

"How can that be, Madame?" I asked. "You inhabit his world—the world of his imagination. Or so you have shown us."

"Ah, Doctor, do we at all times see all those who inhabit our world, whether imaginary *or* solid? As I said, I would be visible to Dr. Doyle only if he were to enter that world while thinking of me. With the imagination, dear friends, it is a case of…"

"… out of mind, out of sight."

"You have it, Mr. Holmes."

"Madame, would you be so good as to…" Holmes indicated that she should lift the necklace. She did so and held it out. The ornament dangled from its chain. "Now," Holmes said, "I am Dr. Doyle entering the room. What do I see?"

"This object."

"And Miss Adler?"

"No."

"Only that object."

"One would expect."

"In mid-air?!" I exclaimed.

"That, Watson, is my hope. If Dr. Doyle wishes to accept the efficacy of spiritualistic phenomena, I will happily enlist him in the game. Miss Adler, you say that at the séance today, Dr. Doyle was trying to reach his father?"

"His recently deceased father. He was hoping to plead his case regarding you."

"But he reached us instead. Excellent."

"As I said, Mr. Holmes, you've been on his mind, actively … guiltily. And so"—she dangled the amulet—"Madame Eneri had little trouble achieving the spiritualistic manifestation she, rather than Dr. Doyle, desired. Now are you a believer?"

"On the contrary, Madame. Watson and I are more than a 'spiritualistic manifestation.' As you have so eloquently explained, we are creatures of the imagination. I believe in the imagination."

"You, the master of deductive reasoning?"

"Deductive reasoning only eliminates the impossible. Leaving us, once again, the improbable."

"Which is?"

"That so intelligent a man as Dr. Doyle believes in ghosts."

"Ah. And your imagination?"

"Enables me to look at things through his mind. Where I see our salvation. Assuming we make *him* see it. This very evening, in fact, before he is able to finish story number eleven."

"How do we do that, Holmes?" I asked.

"By inducing him to see what he so dearly wants to. Miss Adler spoke of the highly suggestible state of Dr. Doyle's mind. And told us he still wishes to see his father. We will accommodate him."

"How do we do *that*?"

"By completing the circle." Holmes gave me an uncharacteristically mischievous smile. "We will conduct a séance."

"*You*, Holmes?!"

Holmes appeared to be deriving great enjoyment from my incredulity. "That is, we will induce Dr. Doyle to conduct a séance."

"And how will we do *that*?"

Miss Adler picked up the necklace and swung its ornament, wicked anticipation on her face.

Holmes nodded his accord. "I count on your invisibility."

"I hope and pray," the good lady replied.

"But, Holmes," I said, "aren't you forgetting something?"

"What is that?"

"Doyle's father is no longer among us. Surely you, above all, don't expect him to…?" I concluded the preposterous thought by an airy twirling of my hand.

"Aren't *you* forgetting something?" Holmes reached into his pocket and brought out a small leather pouch. I recognized it at once.

"You've found your tobacco, Mr. Holmes."

"The tools of my trade, Miss Adler." He unfolded the pouch. Tucked inside were small tubes of facial colouring, coloured pencils, powder, nose putty, a tiny hand-mirror, scissors, even a neatly folded wig. "Have I not in the past shown myself a master of disguise?"

"Except on one occasion I recall," Miss Adler said. And then, a teasing "'Good night, Mr.—'"

Holmes stopped her with a mock bow, then went to the framed photograph on the wall. "This was on the table when we arrived. A photographic portrait, perhaps, of the person they were attempting to summon?" He looked to Miss Adler.

"It is, Mr. Holmes."

Holmes positioned himself beside the photograph. "A decided likeness, no?"

"No," we both exclaimed.

"There will be." Holmes studied the photograph a half-minute or so, then went to the alcove containing the French windows, whence he summoned me. "I shall require your assistance, old man, if you will." He handed me the mirror, then with a nod to Miss Adler—"all the more for your delight, good lady"—stepped behind the draperies and bade me follow. There he proceeded to apply his facial disguise and his wig, aided by me holding the tiny mirror, catching enough of the light to enable his task.

The undertaking, so familiar to him, took no more than a few minutes. He signalled me to part the draperies, which, with much flair, I did, presenting my transformed colleague to Miss Adler.

"My delight, indeed!" she exclaimed. For not only had Holmes made himself up to look like the photograph, he had managed also to give his face a splendid ghostlike pallor. He gave Miss Adler a pleased nod. I closed the draperies behind him.

He studied the room. "Watson, if you would hold yourself concealed in readiness there." He pointed to the curtained alcove. "And, Miss Adler, if you would be so kind as to stand there"—he indicated a spot at the round table—"exactly where you were as Madame Eneri."

"A game? What fun." She went to the designated place. In her hand was the ornament and neck chain.

"Fun it will be, Miss Adler, if Dr. Doyle's aroused mental state causes him to achieve the manifestation of his father, that person being uppermost in his mind."

"That is how it works, Mr. Holmes."

"And then, Holmes, what will we do?"

"That, Watson, depends on what the good doctor does. Be prepared to take your cues from me. Now, then, we must reproduce this afternoon's séance as precisely as possible. So, Miss Adler, would you be kind enough to indicate exactly where at this table Dr. Doyle and Madame were sitting during that event."

"There and there."

Holmes placed chairs where she pointed.

"And you, Miss Adler, if you'd be so good as to position yourself here, splitting the remaining circumference. To be joined, at the appropriate moment by me, then Watson, thus completing a little spiritualistic circle of our own."

"But, Holmes," I said. "This being a séance around the same table as the earlier one, and Miss Adler at the table—as she was when disguised as Madame Eneri—might that not prompt Dr. Doyle to see her?"

"Excellent thought, Watson, but at this séance Miss Adler will be in her own person—albeit invisible—not that of Madame Eneri. I am confident, therefore, that Dr. Doyle will see neither she who is absent from the scene—Madame Eneri—nor she who is absent from his mind—Miss Adler."

"Brilliant, Mr. Holmes."

"Elementary, Miss Adler."

So saying, Holmes went to the doorway, from where he surveyed the scene—an artist assessing a composition. He came back to the round table and lit the candle, then returned to the doorway and signalled me to extinguish the desk lamp. I did so, which allowed the light of the single candle, now the only source of light in the room, to bring out Holmes's ghostly glow even more strikingly. I then took up my position behind the closed draperies, able to peek out at the proceedings. Holmes signalled Miss Adler to hold the ornament over the table. In the candlelight, it dazzled. Holmes studied the tableau.

"It pleases me. Friends, we are ready."

"Ready for…?" Miss Adler's expression said she knew the answer.

"The arrival of our hosts."

"Who have retired for the night," she reminded Holmes.

"Wonderful," he replied. "Their agitation will be all the greater."

I stepped out from the curtains. "And how do you propose to call them here? I should not think we can rouse them physically."

"No need to. In this, too, dear Madame Doyle has shown the way. Places, everyone."

Miss Adler and I returned to our assigned places, then watched as Holmes took the violin and bow from their case. I smiled. He went to the door. With a flourish, he put the instrument under his chin, raised the bow, and prepared to play. "Oh." He paused. "Must tune it first." He looked at us and read our faces. "No?"

"No!!" Miss Adler and I cried together.

Holmes's amused expression told us he was joking.

"You are in good spirits, Mr. Holmes."

"I certainly hope to be, Miss Adler. Ready, my friends?"

We took our positions.

"The *Barcarole* by Hoffman," Holmes announced. "One of my favourites."

"And of Dr. Doyle's, I assume," said Miss Adler.

"Thus stimulating him all the more to see me when I appear, although"—Holmes gestured to his disguise—"concealed in this form and figure."

With that Holmes stepped outside the study doorway, from where the sound would drift up the stairs, and played the lyrical yet haunting tune. He stopped after a few seconds and listened. Nothing. He played again. Nothing. Again.

This time he heard stirring. At once he laid the violin down on the chair by the door, where it could not be missed, and concealed himself behind the curtains, summoning me to his side.

Miss Adler positioned herself at the round table, facing the door, arm straight out, dangling the ornament in the candlelight. A minute passed. Then we heard, descending the stairs: "Please, my dear, remain upstairs. I'll see to it. It was only the wind, I'm sure."

Dr. Doyle appeared in the doorway, in sleeping robe and pyjamas. "Violin, indeed. It was only the…" He stopped short. "The candle. Lit? How? Who…?" He stared past the candle. "Good heavens. The … the … Madame Eneri's amulet. It…"

At that moment, Miss Adler set the charm gently swinging.

"… is moving! In mid-air! By itself! Oh, good heavens … good heavens! Am I really seeing…?" He looked around wildly, as if for an answer. "Touie! Touie!"

He took a hurried step towards the door, which is when he saw the violin on the chair where Holmes had left it. "Aah!" He jumped as if he had seen a ghost, which in a sense he had. He rushed upstairs.

Holmes and I emerged from the curtains.

"It works," Holmes said, exultant. "He believes. He believes! Oh, the dear fool." My colleague came as close to dancing a jig as ever I could have imagined.

"Did you notice my swinging the amulet, Mr. Holmes?"

"Absolutely inspired. But once more to our posts!"

We started back.

"Wait!" I hurried over to the framed photograph of Charles Doyle, took it from the wall, and set it on the table, where the candle flame lent it an eery aspect.

"Brilliant, Watson."

"Elementary, Holmes."

"Wait!" Holmes touched his face, then pointed to mine. "You too shall glow." He indicated the draperies. "But quickly. They are on their way."

Back behind the draperies we went. Miss Adler, at the table, held out the ornament, where it reflected the candlelight most strikingly. As Holmes began applying makeup to my face, we listened for the arrival of the summoned couple. We did not have long to wait.

"I'm sorry to have brought you downstairs, my dear," came Doyle's voice, "but this is extraordinary. Simply extraordinary. If, indeed, I saw what I thought. If, indeed, you see it as well."

As best I could, I peeked out at the proceedings. The Doyles now stood in the doorway, Madame in nightgown and peignoir, her hair done up for the night. She took in the scene at once. Her mouth fell open; her hand went to her breast.

"Oh, Arthur, Madame Eneri's amulet. I see it. In mid-air."

"As do I. And I see the lit candle."

"Yes. And we heard"—she looked around the room—"the violin." There it lay, nowhere near its case. She hugged her shoulders, as if at a sudden thrill.

"And … and … is that not Father's…?" Dr. Doyle glanced at the spot on the wall where the elder Doyle's photograph should have been. Seeing it no longer there, he took a cautious step to the table, and leaned in to confirm its identity. "Touie, I saw you return it to the wall."

"Yet … here it is again. Who moved it?"

"Who lit the candle?"

"Who played the violin?"

"Who holds the amulet?"

As if cued, Irene Adler let go of the neck chain. The amulet crashed onto the table. The Doyles screamed as one. They clutched each other, frozen for several seconds, then their clutching of each other developed into a touching of themselves.

"We are awake, Arthur."

At that moment, Madame noticed that the glass-fronted bookcase was open. Her gaze went to the desk. There sat the open portfolio of poems. Too full of wonder and delight to speak, she merely pointed at it.

"It is a sign," Doyle said. "There are spirits in this room. Trying to reach us … to tell us something."

Madame Doyle nodded, as did Miss Adler, who ever so slowly slid the chairs out from the table.

"Arthur, the chairs. They are…"

The Doyles clung to each other, enticed by the call to sit.

"… summoning us to the table."

And seduced by it.

"We'd best go."

"We'd best."

"Yes, my dear. I believe the time has come."

Exchanging a fearful but excited glance, they moved to the table and sat.

"Oh, Arthur," said Madame Doyle, a tremor in her voice, "if only Madame Eneri were here to witness this."

Miss Adler nearly burst out laughing, but a moment later was back at the task. She pushed the picture towards Dr. Doyle, who watched, transfixed, as it approached him. Next, she slid the charm towards Madame Doyle, who stared awestruck as it moved in her direction. It stopped and lay temptingly before her. Madame hesitated, then picked it up. Audacious lady!

The pendant now dangled from Madame Doyle's hand. Miss Adler leaned in and started it moving. Madame pulled back in alarm but quickly recovered. Both she and her husband stared hypnotically at the charm swinging from her hand. Doyle now pressed his fingers to the table and signalled his wife to do the same. She pressed her free hand, clutching the necklace with the other.

"Father, is it you? Are you here?" Dr. Doyle waited several seconds. "Father, answer us, please, if you are in this room." Again he waited. "It is I, your son Arthur. I want so much to talk with you." He turned to his wife. "Talk to him, my dear."

"To…?"

"To Father. He was always fond of you."

Still dangling the amulet, Madame said, barely above a whisper, "Charles Doyle, it is your daughter-in-law Louise."

"'Touie,' Father." Doyle gestured to her to try again.

"Your son Arthur and I would so much like to see you. Are you with us?"

They waited a few seconds. No reply. "Take my hand," Dr. Doyle whispered. Madame put down the charm and joined hands with her husband, their free hands still pressed to the table. "Father," Doyle said, "please, give us a sign if you are in our presence."

They waited, breathless. More seconds passed. Miss Adler looked at the draperies, behind which Holmes was still in the process of applying glow to my face. Her concern was evident. I communicated this to Holmes. He stuck out his arm, signalling her to do something, anything, to gain time. She thought a moment, then turned back to the table, leaned in, and blew gently on the candle.

"Arthur, the candle flame. It ripples."

"It is he! Oh, Father, answer us somehow."

Again Miss Adler leaned over the table, and this time knocked on it, slowly and heavily. The Doyles nearly came out of their chairs, to her great delight. For good measure, she once more blew on the flame.

"It is. It *is* he! Oh, Father, can you show yourself?"

They waited, poised to see whatever. As did Miss Adler. Again Holmes signalled her to keep things going, which surprised me, for he had finished my makeup. I could feel the tension in the room growing. Is that what Holmes was about? Miss Adler pondered, uncertain what to do.

Doyle came to her aid. "Father, is it truly you? If so, move the candle flame again."

Miss Adler leaned in and blew on the flame. It rippled.

"Truly, it is," Doyle whispered to Madame, his excitement palpable.

But still no appearance from Holmes, who stood beside me calm and composed, apparently waiting for what he deemed the perfect moment. The moment of maximum accessibility to Dr. Doyle's suggestible mind? Whatever, an increasingly distressed Miss Adler thought a moment, then moved behind the Doyles, and blew softly on the back of Dr. Doyle's neck.

"Oh, Father, I feel your presence."

Then Madame Doyle's neck.

"And I."

Doctor and Madame exchanged looks of absolute euphoria. "Please, Father," Doyle implored, "will you not appear to us?"

All waited. Miss Adler, after a pleading glance towards Holmes and me, picked up the photograph of Charles Doyle, and as the Doyles watched stupefied, floated it from the table towards its spot on the wall, by way of the draperies. A fortuitous route, for as she was about to pass by, Holmes nodded that the moment had arrived. I parted the curtains, and out of their shadowy folds stepped the elder Doyle, in full ghostliness. I closed the curtains behind him, leaving myself concealed but able to watch all.

Dr. Doyle saw the spectre immediately; Madame Doyle, by virtue, I daresay, of her intimate bond with her husband, saw it a bare moment later. The vision rendered both of them fairly beside themselves with something akin to ecstasy.

Miss Adler had remained by the alcove, and was now holding the picture close beside Holmes's face, as if for comparison with my colleague's ghostly rendition. Deftly Holmes took it from her, held it there a moment, then pushed it toward the Doyles, by way of declaring a likeness between the portrait and himself, and thereby announcing his identity. He then returned the photograph to Miss Adler, via whose invisible self it floated across the room and back onto its spot on the wall. Meanwhile, Holmes held himself in the half-shadow beyond the immediate circle of candlelight, no doubt not yet willing to test his disguise fully.

"Oh, Father ... Father. Is it really you?"

Holmes nodded.

"Do you have something to tell us? Is that why you have come?"

Holmes nodded.

"Can you speak?"

Holmes indicated nothing.

"Should I ask you questions?"

Holmes nodded.

"Are you in pain?"

Holmes shook his head.

"Are you happy where you are?"

Holmes hesitated a moment, then shrugged noncommittally.

"Do you know we are moving to Switzerland?"

Holmes indicated nothing.

"Louise and I, Father, we are moving to Switzerland. We leave in a few days."

Still Holmes did not react.

"Swit-zer-land," Doyle said. "The Alps. Where the air is clean."

Holmes shook his head sadly.

"*Because* the air is clean. For Louise's health, Father."

Holmes shook his head.

"Do you not approve? Do you say no to that?"

Again Holmes shook his head.

"You *do* say no? Or do you say no, you are not saying no? That is, yes."

Holmes deliberated.

"Ask 'yes' questions, Arthur," Madame whispered. "Ask if he wants me to be cured."

"Father, do you want your daughter-in-law Louise to be cured?"

Holmes nodded.

"Do you see that we must get her out of England, then?"

Holmes nodded.

"To Switzerland."

Holmes nodded, then shook his head sadly. A second time. A third.

"What is it, Father? Yes to Switzerland?"

Holmes nodded.

"But no to Switzerland?"

Holmes considered, then nodded.

"Arthur, ask him how it can be no and yes at the same time."

"You said only yes questions."

"I fear we've exhausted those. Ask for a sign."

Doyle emitted a frustrated sigh. I must admit that I myself was having difficulty interpreting some of Holmes's responses. "Father," Doyle said, "we are confused. You approve of Switzerland, yet disapprove of it. Can you give us a sign?"

Holmes pantomimed pen across paper.

"Writing? Something about writing?"

Holmes nodded.

"You want me to write something?"

Holmes hesitated.

"You want me *not* to write something?"

Holmes shook his head vigorously.

"Ah, you want me *not* to not write. To write, in other words."

"Arthur, this is hardly the time for puns," Madame whispered.

Holmes pointed to Madame Doyle and repeated the gesture of writing.

"Something about Louise and writing? Write *about* her."

Holmes shook his head. He thought a moment, then mimed coughing, then caressing someone.

"Ah, take care of Louise—take care of Louise's illness."

Miss Adler applauded, as did I. Holmes nodded and repeated the writing motion.

"Take care of Louise … and also write. Is that it, Father?"

Holmes nodded.

"Write what?"

Holmes made a rolling motion with his hands.

Doyle appeared puzzled.

"Arthur," Madame whispered, "I think he wants you to *go on* writing."

Holmes nodded vigorously.

"Oh, Father, I will, I will. I will help to cure Touie, and I will also keep writing. But, Father, not what I've been writing. I intend to—"

Holmes abruptly raised a hand, then shook his head sternly.

"No? That's not it?"

Holmes repeated the rolling gesture.

"Yes, Father, I've got that. But write what?"

Holmes jabbed his palm emphatically. Doyle mimicked the action, trying to fathom its meaning.

"Father," Madame Doyle said, "can you give us another sign? What is it Arthur should go on writing? Can you tell us? What is it Arthur should…?"

"Oh, dear, I hope it's not…" Doyle's worried frown completed the sentence.

Out of mind out of sight? If so, *in* mind…

My moment had arrived.

Holmes stamped his foot twice, our pre-arranged signal. From the alcove, I gave two answering knocks, then a third. With a flourish, I parted the draperies and made my entrance, my right hand pointing accusingly at Doyle, in my left my walking stick held high, Zeus about to hurl a thunderbolt. The gentleman rose in what must have been twofold terror at my appearance: my sudden appearance on the scene, and the glowing appearance of my face. Miss Adler clapped in glee.

At the sight of me, Madame Doyle gripped the table. Her husband sat frozen, slack-jawed, pinned to his chair by my accusatory finger. But after several seconds, he managed to give his head a hard shake. "No! It cannot be! I am done with you! Done with you, do you hear?! *Can* you hear?!" At a loss what to do, I could only nod glumly. "Forever!" Doyle continued. "Leave my thoughts! Haunt me no more!"

He turned away in anguish. Stung by his words, yet moved by his obvious distress, I looked to Holmes for instructions. He gestured me to remain calm and discreetly motioned to Miss Adler to come over. Surreptitiously, he whispered something to her. She went to the desk.

"Why … *why* did you bring him, Father?" Doyle cried.

Holmes pointed to the desk. The doctor and his wife looked there, to see the green folder emerge from beneath the pile of papers and float into my hand. At a signal from my spectral colleague, I raised it and shook it angrily at Doyle.

"What are you trying to say?" he asked. I hesitated, unsure how to answer. Fortunately, the doctor charged ahead. "Do you accuse me?"

Solemnly I nodded.

"Of what do you accuse me?"

I brought my fist down on the folder.

"Why do you torment me with that?" he cried. "I have no choice. My wife—my beloved wife—is ill. I have neglected her while sustaining you and Mr. Holmes—"

Madame laid a hand on her husband's sleeve. "No, Arthur, you mustn't…"

But the doctor was not listening. His attention was all on me. "No more! Now I devote myself only to her. To her! Do you understand what it is to have a wife one loves?" Again his words stung, which he must have seen, for at once he said, "Yes … yes, of course you do, old man. My apologies. But surely, then, you understand my feelings. Can you not sympathize with me?"

Before I could think to reply, he was on to a new thought. "By the way, what are you doing here alone? I never let you go anywhere alone. Home by wife and fireside, perhaps, when Holmes comes fetching you away on a case—you, too, you see, the neglectful husband."

I recoiled as if struck. Could it be?

"Come to think of it, Father," Doyle said to the spectre, "where *is* Holmes? If you brought Watson, why not Holmes as well?"

A question none of us had foreseen. Holmes looked at me blankly, then at Miss Adler. We returned blank looks of our own. Dr. Doyle looked pleased.

At that moment, Madame Doyle half-rose from her chair and fixed her eyes in turn on the violin, the bookcase, the folder of poems, and then the room itself, nodding at each as if doing sums. She ended by settling her calculating gaze on the ghostly figure of her father-in-law.

"After all," Doyle went on, "is it not Holmes himself who should be pleading for his life? To no avail, I might add."

This was not the direction in which Holmes desired matters to proceed. I saw, and shared, his uncertainty. Our consternation multiplied when Dr. Doyle said, "Father, please summon Holmes. Gladly would I explain to him why I must do this. He is an intelligent, reasonable man."

The spectre was obliged to nod agreement.

"He would understand."

To this, the spectre was noncommittal.

"Summon him, please."

Doyle waited long seconds, until at last he threw up his hands and turned to me. "Dr. Watson, you come in vain. I can no longer give you and Holmes the attention you are accustomed to." Then back to the spectre. "Father, I am deeply sorry that your visit, so fervently sought, must turn out this way."

Could this be a ruse? I wondered. I looked to Holmes; it appeared from his narrowed stare that he was wondering the same thing. Had Doyle seen through our disguises, seen through the magical doings, seen though the whole charade? Holmes continued to study him. No, I saw him decide, it's simply intransigence. Recalcitrant, bull-headed intransigence. The man will not be moved.

A clear impasse. Dr. Doyle sensed it. Madame Doyle sensed it. Holmes and I both sensed it. As for Irene Adler…

She pressed the finger of one hand on the finger of the other, a clear sign to Holmes and me: it is time for Dr. Doyle's characters to press their writing fingers on his.

She touched the amulet where it lay on the table and held her hand there. "Arthur … Conan … Doyle," she intoned, her voice resounding through the room.

At once, any obstinacy on Doyle's part vanished, converted into sheer hair-prickling fright. For the second time that evening, he and his wife clutched each other, terrified by this voice from thin air. Even Holmes and I were taken aback by it, albeit happily so.

"Arthur … Conan … Doyle," Miss Adler repeated in a lugubrious tone. She took her hand from the amulet, as if no longer needing it. "Heed … your … father." She glanced at Holmes, and more for his benefit than Doyle's, laid a pointed emphasis on each word. "Heed. Your. Father."

"That voice," Doyle muttered.

Miss Adler gestured to Holmes, this time moving fingers and thumb together rapidly several times, urging Charles Doyle to, for Heaven's sake, *talk*! Still Holmes held back. Did he not understand? With an impatient parting glare, Miss Adler turned back to Doyle. "*Hearken* to your father." As before, her words, though directed at the doctor, were clearly intended for my colleague.

"I know that voice," Doyle murmured. "I have heard it before. Who the deuce…?"

"*Hearken*," Miss Adler repeated, even more pointedly, "to what your father *says*." She threw Holmes an exasperated look and repeated her talk gesture, even more graphically urgent.

A moment passed, then at last, from the spectre's mouth came "Ar … thur," the tone heavy, tomb-like.

The Doyles were gripped with new astonishment.

"… Co … nan," Miss Adler intoned.

"… Doy …el," I chanted.

Holmes took a step forward and continued in the same sepulchral tone. "Hearken to my words."

"Yes, Father?"

"You … must … not … do … this … thing."

"What thing?"

"*You know what thing*!!" Holmes raged. The Doyles shrank. "The crime you are planning. Murder. Murder most foul."

"Father, please believe me, it is not—"

Holmes raised his hand. "I see deep within. A chasm. A bottomless chasm, a cataract, the rushing of water."

Miss Adler began to make rushing-water sounds. The spectre nodded slowly, as if in solemn acceptance of the supporting sound. I managed a discreet thumbs-up.

"I see two men struggling at the edge," Holmes said. "One is our beloved detective, the other … wait, his image is fleeting … he … is…"

"A-a-ye-rish," I chanted.

"Aye. A-a-ye-rish," chimed Holmes. "Ye-e-e-s. An Irish … professor. Professor M. For murder, my son. You are giving free rein to murder."

"No, no, Father. M for Moriarty."

"*Murder*, Arthur."

"And … he is only a means to an end. He, too, will perish in the…"

Up went Holmes's hand. "Do *not* contradict your father. You cannot—you *must* not—do this thing."

"What are you saying, Father? Oh, dear."

"I am saying your detective must live. His associate, this good doctor, must remain at his side."

"We must go on investigating crime," I said.

"Solving the unsolvable," said the spectre.

"Helping persons in distress." My abandonment to the charade seemed to have released whatever modest complement of inventiveness I possessed. I was finding it an agreeably novel and liberating experience.

"Then help *us*, Father," Doyle pleaded, "for *we* are in distress. Louise in distress over her health, I in distress over her. You yourself have acknowledged that. Are the needs of Holmes, a mere literary figure, greater than those of a real human being?"

"*Mere*?" exclaimed Holmes. "Not mere, Arthur. A grand creation, rather." I saw Miss Adler beaming. "And, my son," the spectre continued, "in the world which he inhabits, Holmes *is* a real human being."

"Watson," Doyle said, "I appeal to you, as one doctor to another. There is illness here."

"And I to you," I replied, "as one writer to another. There is invention here."

"No, great malady!"

"Great mystery."

"Consumption, Dr. Watson!"

"Imagination, Dr. Doyle! It gave—gives—us life."

"At what cost?" Doyle looked glumly at his wife. "That alone is enough to damn me."

"Speak not of damnation, please," Holmes said in his most crypt-like voice yet.

"Then what of guilt, Father? Mine. Can you not feel for your son?"

"Can *you* not, Arthur?" replied Holmes.

"I?"

"Are you not father to Holmes? And to Watson? And to all your 'mere literary figures?'"

"That's true, Arthur," Madame Doyle whispered. "They are your children."

"Holmes is more than that," the spectre said.

"More, Father?" said Doyle, a trace of apprehension in his voice. "What more?"

Holmes held out his hand, into which Miss Adler floated the slipper holding Doyle's tobacco. Holmes set it before Doyle.

"How embarrassing, Arthur," Madame whispered.

"I fail to see what this—" Dr. Doyle was stopped by his father's placing before him, as if in ritual, the coal scuttle full of cigars, which Holmes's acolyte Miss Adler had brought to him.

"Ah, my dear," said Madame Doyle, "I knew you would one day regret your slovenly ways."

"I regret nothing, Touie. And I do not see why Father is…" Doyle stopped again. This time he saw the Beecher photograph move through the air from the mantel to his father's hands, which solemnly set it before him. As Doyle tried to fathom what all this might mean, he saw the jack-knifed correspondence lift itself from the mantel, travel to his father, and alight on the table. At this point I entered the fray, taking Doyle's walking stick from the umbrella stand and setting it among the other items. Our solemn rite reached its apotheosis when Miss Adler, who had slipped out of the room, entered carrying an outer garment like the one she had donned that afternoon as Madame Eneri.

"My Ulster?!" Doyle exclaimed. "It, too, floating in mid-air?"

Miss Adler circled the Doyles twice, before fluttering the Ulster like a toreador enticing the bull.

"What? How?" And then it came to him. "*My* Ulster? No. *Hers. Both*?? And … the voice. So long ago. Of course! The slim youth in the Ulster! Is it…?"

And suddenly, *voilà*—if I may borrow from our cross-channel neighbours—there, now firmly in her creator's mind, stood the resplendent Irene Adler.

"It is!" Doyle exclaimed. "You! The young man in my Ulster!"

"Young woman," Miss Adler said.

"Here again."

"Here still."

Madame Doyle held her breath, as if fearing that to utter a word would shatter this sacred moment. Miss Adler settled the garment onto the table among the other paraphernalia and stepped back. Dr. Doyle, trying to reason it out, touched each object tentatively, reverently.

At that moment was heard the *Barcarole* by Hofmann. As the ghostly Holmes played, he moved towards Doyle, then abruptly stopped playing and laid the violin before him. Doyle touched his head in what appeared to be a mixture of amazement and fear. He clamped his other hand onto the violin, as if to stifle it, but at once jerked it away, as from a hot surface. With both hands he sliced the air, a gesture that screamed, "Stop!" He shook his head vigorously, clearly distraught by great turmoil occurring there. He took some moments to calm himself.

"The music, Touie. What did you make of the—?"

"I never knew your father played the violin." Madame's expression showed her earlier scepticism and calculation.

"He never did. But, Touie, who played after?"

"After?"

"After Father put down the instrument."

Madame Doyle looked at her husband with concern. "Who played what?"

"The music!"

"The music?"

"Did you not hear it? The violin?"

"*After* Father?"

"Yes, Touie."

"Did you?"

"Yes, Touie."

"No."

"No?"

"Arthur, I heard music only while the instrument was being played."

"Touie"—again Doyle touched his head—"what is going on in here?"

"I don't know. But I can tell you what is going on out *here*." She indicated the articles on the table. "These. They are all your things."

"My things."

"And *his* things." She gave him a moment. "At one and the same time."

"And ..."

"... music, Arthur..."

"… without being played …"

"… which only you heard."

"Well, my son," said the spectre, whom the Doyles, in their mutual bafflement, had been ignoring, "this case is not without its points of interest."

Doyle stared at his father, no doubt taken aback at hearing him speak these familiar words. He turned his gaze to the violin, there on the table with the other items, then back to his father. A look of dismay swept his face.

"Whose music, my son?" coaxed the spectre.

Doyle struggled with the question. "Whose…?"

"Better, *where* is the music?"

"Where … is the music?" Doyle spoke as in a daze.

"Where has it always been?" the spectre insisted. "Whose are these items, 'at one and the same time?'"

Doyle lowered his eyes, as if to peer inward. His face went from dark mystification, as he struggled to grasp the import of these phenomena, to a slowly dawning perception. "Oh, no." His tone was more of a bleat than a cry.

Holmes read it perfectly. "So, Arthur, can you kill Holmes?"

Doyle sank in his chair. "Can I kill myself? Oh, dear God. What am I to do?"

"Holmes cannot die," said the spectre, "for he lives in Arthur. *As* Arthur. Arthur sees that now. Does he not?"

Doyle hesitated, uncertain.

"Your poem, dear," Madame Doyle whispered, and pointed to the desk.

Doyle looked there and saw his leather-bound portfolio. He drew in a slow breath and nodded sadly. "Yes, Father, Arthur sees that now." He paused a moment, in deepest thought, out of which came, "Yet, Father, Holmes cannot live, for Arthur no longer wants to breathe life into him. Holmes sees *that* now, surely."

"I … suppose he does, surely."

"What am I to do?!"

Miss Adler, clever lady, had the answer. "Use Holmes's method."

"Synthetic or analytic?" Doyle said wearily, his sense of helplessness visible.

"The evidence at hand," she replied. "Evidence you yourself have created. In this case, by omission." She picked up the green folder and extracted one of the pages, which she handed to me. She pointed to a spot. "Read, Dr. Watson."

"'*The path*,'" I read, "'*had been cut halfway round the falls to afford a complete view, but it ends abruptly, and the traveller has to return as he came. We had turned to do so, when we saw a Swiss lad come running along it with a letter in his hand. It bore the mark of the hotel which we had just left and was addressed to me…*'"

I looked at Dr. Doyle and pointed an inquiring finger at myself.

"Yes, you, Watson," he said.

"… '*addressed to me by the landlord. It appeared that within a very few minutes of our leaving, an English lady had arrived who was in the very last stages of consumption.*'"

Madame Doyle let out a gasp. Doyle took her hand. "Quite all right, my dear. Just artistic license, as you shall see. Read, Watson."

"'*She was journeying now to join friends at Lucerne, when a sudden hemorrhage had overtaken her. It was thought that she could hardly live a few hours…*'"

"Not you, my dear," Doyle exclaimed to Madame. "I promise you."

"Read, Watson," said Miss Adler.

"… '*but it would be a great consolation to her to see an English doctor, and, if I would only return, etc … It was impossible to refuse the request of a fellow countrywoman dying in a strange land.*'"

Madame Doyle's hand went to her heart. "Oh, Arthur."

"No!" Doyle shouted. "Finish, Doctor!"

"I have heard enough, my son," Holmes said. "The rest is not relevant."

"It is to me!" Doyle clutched his wife's hand. "To us!"

Holmes sighed, resigned to this unfortunate suspension of the pursuit. "Read on, Dr. Watson."

"'*It may have been a little over an hour before I reached the hotel. The landlord was standing at the porch. "Well," said I, as I came hurrying up, "I trust that she is no worse?" A look of surprise passed over his face, and at the first quiver of his eyebrows my heart turned to lead in my breast.*'"

I looked up, totally taken with the story, though it was not mine—or not yet. "It's quite good, isn't it?" *I must be allowed to write this*, I thought. *Minus the nasty business as regards Holmes, of course.*

"Continue, man, continue!" Doyle exclaimed. "One more line." He glanced at his wife, on his face benign anticipation.

I read. "'"*You did not write this?*" *I said, pulling the letter from my pocket. "There is no sick Englishwoman in the hotel?" "Certainly not!" he cried.*'"

"Stop!" Doyle turned to Madame and looked at her with as tender an expression as I had ever seen on a man's face. "'No sick Englishwoman.' My wish, my dream, Touie, for you."

Dr. Doyle and Madame looked at each other as if, for the moment, nothing else existed. I suspect that for them at that moment nothing else did.

"Enough, I say," Holmes interjected. "We have enough."

"Oh, no," Madame murmured, her soft eyes lingering on her husband. "Not nearly."

"Thank you, Miss Adler," Holmes said. "Yet again have you shown the way." Then, to Doyle: "Arthur, why is Dr. Watson called away thus from the falls?"

The question wrenched Doyle from his and his wife's mutual immersion. "You heard, Father. Because he receives the false note telling him…"

"No, my son. Let me rephrase the question: Why do you *have him* called away from the falls?"

"The note has been written by Professor Moriarty…"

Hearing from Doyle's mouth the name of the wraith we had banished, Holmes staggered a moment, but managed to pull himself up at once. Had Doyle noticed?

"… who," Doyle continued, "wishes to remove from the scene any possible witness to the crime he is about to commit."

"Oh?" Holmes said. "This 'Napoleon of crime,' about to murder Holmes, would be deterred by Dr. Watson's presence? He cannot deal with Watson as well?"

"I should think not," I interjected.

"What was in your mind *really*," the spectre said to Doyle, "when you wrote that? When you removed Watson from the scene?"

"I … I …" Doyle strove to answer, then shook his head. "I am sure you are going to tell me."

"I am, Arthur. But first I will tell you that you are correct. There must be no witness. For, my son, I alone see into the chasm, where I discover *why* this writer"—he pointed to Doyle—"has decided there must be no witness."

"For Heaven's sake," Madame Doyle exclaimed, "please stop hinting and tell us!"

"Yes," said Doyle and I.

Miss Adler raised her hand, an eager schoolgirl with the correct answer.

"Miss Adler?" said Holmes.

"There must be no witness … because there is to be no crime."

"What?!!" cried Doyle, looking ready for combat.

Holmes ignored him. "You have it, dear child," he said, obviously enjoying his patriarchal role. Miss Adler replied with a curtsey.

"No crime, Arthur," Holmes repeated. "A deception only. Dr. Watson is called away so there will be no witness to the fact that after their fierce struggle at the edge of the precipice, this … this …" Holmes hesitated getting the name out. Again he glanced to see if Doyle had noticed.

"… this Moriarty," Miss Adler said.

"… is supposedly … supposedly … propelled into the cataract below," Holmes said. "But…" He deferred to Miss Adler.

"Holmes is not."

"Holmes is *not*?!!" said Doyle.

"Holmes is not," the great detective repeated.

"Holmes is spared," Miss Adler said.

"As he must be," Holmes concluded.

"But if true, Father," Madame Doyle said, "why would Arthur want Dr. Watson to be ignorant of the fact?"

"Why, indeed?" I asked.

"Why, indeed?" Holmes said. "Because…"

"Because…" said Doyle, nodding sadly, as if starting to understand.

"Because Holmes…" said Miss Adler.

"Doyle…" said the good doctor.

"… needs a rest," said he and Holmes together, Holmes quietly triumphant, Doyle pained and spent.

"And if anyone," said Holmes, "*anyone…*"

"… save brother Mycroft…" said Dr. Doyle.

"… and especially," suggested Miss Adler, "dear, dear Dr. Watson…"

"…knows Holmes is alive," Doyle said, "it will be…"

"… found out," said Holmes, "and Holmes…"

"… Doyle…" said the doctor.

"… will be…"

"… put back to work…"

"… solving the crimes of Europe…"

"… *concocting* the crimes of Europe." Dr. Doyle shook his head at the sorry realization.

"Q.E.D." concluded my brilliant colleague, with a considerable measure of satisfaction.

"Well reasoned, Father … Miss Adler," said Doyle, clearly impressed despite himself.

"Elementary, Arthur," said Holmes.

Dr. Doyle took his wife's hand. He nodded solemnly, resigned to the momentous truth. "Father is right, my dear. I am weary. Weary of Holmes—sorry, Father—weary of Watson"—he offered me an apologetic gesture—"weary of the entire collection and concoction. And weary, dearest, of this constant helpless anxiety over you. I simply cannot go on as I have."

"Nor can Holmes," the spectre said. "Nor should he. Nor need he."

"What is the solution, Father?"

"A holiday, for you and for Holmes."

"A holiday?"

"Yours is already arranged. As for Holmes…"

"Yes?"

"He has long desired a voyage abroad."

"He has?"

"Yes, my son. To the Orient."

"The East?"

"Near and Far."

"I see."

"Tibet has always held its attractions. The monasteries there fascinate him."

"You know this?"

"Oh, yes. And then, perhaps, a stop in southern Europe on the way back."

"When would that be?"

"He would depart straight from Reichenbach. As you and Louise arrive in Switzerland, he would be leaving. Rather neat, eh?"

"No, Father, I meant … you said 'on the way back.' When do you propose *that* would be?"

"That is yet to be decided. Dependent, perhaps, on the state of weariness of the traveller."

"My own, as well?"

"Is there a difference?"

Doyle shook his head and sighed.

"You and Louise," Holmes continued, "her health restored—my fondest wish for you, beloved daughter-in-law—shall one day return to England, to this empty house, to resume your life here. And so shall Holmes."

"To this empty house?"

"Or some other."

"And once the world traveller has returned to England?" Doyle asked. "What then?"

"I imagine much unsolved crime will have accumulated."

"Perhaps, Father, the traveller will no longer wish to participate in such matters. A quieter life may hold its attractions. After the Tibetan monasteries, you understand."

"All things are possible."

"Including," said a happy Madame Doyle, who, like Miss Adler and myself, had been fascinated by this last exchange between her husband and his ghostly father, "that we are at last agreed? Arthur?"

Doyle gave his wife an affectionate smile. "Agreed. Dr. Watson?"

"Agreed. Miss Adler?"

"For the 'collection and concoction,' agreed." She turned to the spectre. "Charles Doyle?"

"Agreed. I know I speak for Holmes, as well."

At this, Madame Doyle let out a barely subdued scoff. Holmes glanced at her with a pleased expression.

"Indeed," said Doyle, looking pleased himself.

"Well," Madame said, "that's settled then."

"And now, my son," said Holmes, reverting to his sepulchral tone, which— without its having been noticed by anyone—had been abandoned over the last many minutes, "it is time for me to return to the place whence I came. Farewell."

"Farewell … Father. Thank you for coming."

"And I must depart, as well," I said.

"And I," added Miss Adler, slipping the charm necklace into her reticule. "With Dr. Doyle's assistance, of course."

"But with the greatest regret, dear lady."

"Thank you, Doctor. Good night to you and to Madame Doyle. Do think of me from time to time."

"Most assuredly, my dear."

And so," said the Doyles, "good night, Miss Adler, Dr. Watson."

Doyle gave me a small wave. "Do give my regards to Holmes, Doctor. Tell him he missed a jolly good séance."

Madame Doyle gave her husband a sceptical look. On his face, she saw the hint of a smile.

"Pity," I said. "It might have made a believer of him."

Miss Adler and I exchanged farewells, then with my walking stick I signalled to Holmes that I was ready for our departure. He held up a hand, bidding me wait. Quite deliberately, he turned to Dr. Doyle and offered him a slow, respectful bow, in its trail an uncustomary look of affection. I felt as he, and did the same. A moment later, Miss Adler joined us in the gesture. Dr. Doyle acknowledged our homage with a deferential nod of his own and an expression that I read only as genuine fondness.

Holmes now went to Miss Adler and she to him. "Good night ... dear lady." She offered her hand. He held it a long moment, then bent and kissed it. Reluctantly he let it go and proceeded to the French windows, where I joined him. Miss Adler remained a short distance away. About to leave, Holmes stopped, turned to her once more, as I knew he must, and as she knew he would. They exchanged a last warm look.

"Good night," she said, "Mr—"

A quick but decisive gesture from Dr. Doyle stopped her. Instead, she blew a kiss to Holmes and vanished from the room, on her way, I assumed, to rejoin her fellow retirees—the 'collection and concoction.' Dr. Doyle and Madame joined hands, as if still in the grip of the séance, Doyle looking off with what I would call a very satisfied grin. Did he actually mouth the words "Mr. Sherlock Holmes?" We shall never know, for at that moment Holmes and I were off and away, whisked down the street we'd travelled that afternoon, back to 221B then Reichenbach and whatever the future might hold.

But I suspect that immediately upon our departure, Dr. Doyle eyed the green folder waiting for the morrow, kissed Madame, blew out the candle, and with his dear wife on his arm proceeded contentedly up the stairs, to resume the sleep so fortuitously interrupted.

END

ABOUT THE AUTHOR

Maurice Breslow has spent his professional life as a stage director, playwright, and author. A graduate of Cornell, Tufts, and Yale School of Drama, he has published stories in the Queen's Quarterly, Kingston Whig-Standard Magazine, and Readers' Digest, and his plays have been produced at theatres in Canada and the United States. In 1997, his play *Suffer the Children* won the Canadian National Jewish Playwriting Contest.

Maurice is an avid birdwatcher, photographer, reader of fiction and non-fiction, and student of the piano, which he took up as an adult years ago. He and his wife Margaret—a singer and teacher of voice—enjoy canoeing and camping near their home just north of Kingston, Ontario, which they share with their affectionate cat Millie. The couple have a son, Max, who lives with his wife in New York City, and a daughter, Miriam, in Halifax.

www.ingramcontent.com/pod-product-compliance
Lightning Source LLC
Chambersburg PA
CBHW031342060726
47590CB00007B/2591